TRIUMPHANT LOVE
A CHRISTIAN ROMANCE

JULIETTE DUNCAN

BOOK 4 "THE TRUE LOVE SERIES"

PRAISE FOR "TRIUMPHANT LOVE"

"Couldn't put this down! Wonderful conclusion to book series." *Paula*

"This book really makes you stop and think about being faithful to God. Love the characters. " *Love to Read*

"It was very inspiring and realistic. It helped me see things from a better perspective. I recommend it to anyone." *Alexandra*

"This book was a wonderfully satisfying conclusion to Juliet Duncan's True Love series. It is so encouraging to read novels written from a Christ centered perspective. Of characters who put God first and really seek -- and trust -- that He will work out His perfect will in their lives. My heartfelt thanks to the author.." *tinycamper*

ALSO BY JULIETTE DUNCAN

Find all of Juliette Duncan's books on her website:
www.julietteduncan.com/library

True Love Series
Tender Love
Tested Love
Tormented Love
Triumphant Love

Precious Love Series
Forever Cherished
Forever Faithful
Forever His

Water's Edge Series
When I Met You
Because of You
With You Beside Me
All I Want is You
It Was Always You
My Heart Belongs to You

A Sunburned Land Series
A mature-age romance series
Slow Road to Love
Slow Path to Peace
Slow Ride Home

Slow Dance at Dusk
Slow Trek to Triumph
Christmas at Goddard Downs

The Shadows Series

A jilted teacher, a charming Irishman, & the chance to escape
their pasts & start again.

Lingering Shadows
Facing the Shadows
Beyond the Shadows
Secrets and Sacrifice
A Highland Christmas

A Time For Everything Series

A mature-age Christian Romance series

A Time to Treasure
A Time to Care
A Time to Abide
A Time to Rejoice

Transformed by Love Christian Romance Series

Because We Loved
Because We Forgave
Because We Dreamed
Because We Believed
Because We Cared

Billionaires with Heart Series

Her Kind-Hearted Billionaire
Her Generous Billionaire

Her Disgraced Billionaire
Her Compassionate Billionaire

The Potter's House Books...
Stories of hope, redemption, and second chances.
The Homecoming
Unchained
Blessings of Love
The Hope We Share
The Love Abounds
Love's Healing Touch
Melody of Love
Whispers of Hope
Promise of Peace

Heroes Of Eastbrooke Christian Suspense Series
Safe in His Arms
Under His Watch
Within His Sight
Freed by His Love

Stand Alone Christian Romantic Suspense
Leave Before He Kills You

The Madeleine Richards Series
Although the 3 book series is intended mainly for pre-teen/Middle Grade girls, it's been read and enjoyed by people of all ages.

CHAPTER 1

*H*unters Hollow, Montana

JAYDEN WILLIAMS WAS STOCKING shelves when a flash of red caught his eye. *Angie!* He smiled to himself. This was a bonus— he hadn't expected to see her until the weekend. He jumped off the ladder and wiped his hands on a rag and waited for her to reach him. The last few weeks had been amazing. His heart beat faster every time he thought about their first kiss, and he still couldn't believe that Angie Morgan had agreed to be his girlfriend. Her red hair and green eyes were the last thing he thought about before going to sleep every night, and the first thing on his mind every morning. He couldn't get her out of his head. He didn't want to.

And now here she was, but something wasn't right. She didn't look herself, her eyes weren't sparkling and there was a trace of sadness to her usually happy face. What was wrong? Surely she wasn't about to break up with him? Everything had been going so well.

"Angie, nice to see you." He tried not to sound worried.

"Hey Jayden." Her voice had lost its spark.

"Didn't expect to see you today." He shoved his hands in his pockets.

"Can you take a break?"

His heart raced. Something was wrong. He checked the time. Five minutes until lunch break. Charmian would let him go early. "Sure."

He followed Angie to a quiet café in the mall. He'd brought his own lunch to work, so he just ordered a soda. Angie ordered the same. She sat opposite him, fiddling with her straw. He hadn't dared ask why she wanted to see him, but he had a strong feeling she didn't want to go out with him anymore. It puzzled him, because just last Sunday he'd gone to church with her for the first time, and she'd held his hand right through the service. And her parents had accepted him. Well, he thought they had. So, what had changed?

"Jayden, I need to tell you something before you hear it from someone else."

His head jerked up. Did she have another boyfriend? Was she sick? "Hear what, Ange?" He gulped.

She held his gaze; her bottom lip quivered slightly.

He reached out and took her hand. "Tell me, Angie. I can take it." *I can't, but I need to know.*

She let out the smallest chuckle. "Oh Jayden. It's not you. It's... it's Jessica." Her body stiffened as her expression sobered even further. "She's... she's pregnant."

Jayden straightened. "Pregnant? Your sister?"

Angie leaned forward and held her finger to her lips. "Shh…"

"Sorry." Jayden lowered his voice and glanced around. "She can't be."

Angie let out a heavy sigh. "She is. And the whole town's about to know."

"Can't she do something about it?"

Angie pulled back. "Jayden! How could you ask such a question?"

Yes, how could he? Of course Angie's parents wouldn't even hear of it. "Sorry. That was dumb."

"School starts next Monday, and Dad's making an announcement at the school staff meeting today, so word's going to get around real quick."

Jayden's forehead puckered. "Why would he do that? Surely he'd want to keep it quiet."

"That's what I thought, but he said it's better they find out from him than hear it as gossip."

Jayden shook his head. *Amazing.* If it was him, he'd probably want to keep it quiet as long as he could.

"How is she? And what about her boyfriend and his parents?"

Angie began fiddling with her straw again. "Oh, Blake's parents are livid. They've disowned him. Mom and Dad have taken him in until he goes off to College at the end of the week."

Jayden sat back in his chair. "Wow, I can't imagine my dad doing that. He'd probably be like Blake's dad and kick me out."

"No he wouldn't, not from what you've told me about him."

Jayden shrugged. "Maybe." The letter he'd got from Dad last week had almost made him pack up and catch the next flight home. He probably would have, if it hadn't been for Angie.

He sipped his soda. "A baby, huh?"

Angie's eyes misted over.

Jayden sighed. Why'd he say that? "I'm sorry. It must be hard on all of you."

Angie sniffed and nodded. "I just feel so sorry for Jess." Her body shuddered as tears rolled down her cheeks. "And finishing school's going to be hard."

"She'll keep going for a while, won't she?"

Angie nodded. "As long as she can. And after that, she can study online."

"And your parents are being really good about it?"

A soft smile grew on her face. "Yes, they've been amazing."

"You're very lucky to have parents like that."

"I know. Most parents would have got really angry. They're sad, but they're okay."

Jayden finished his drink and checked the time. "I need to get back to work, Angie, but can we catch up sometime soon?"

"Yes, I'd like that." She picked up her purse and then angled her head. "Come to Bible Study with me tomorrow night? We could hang out afterwards…"

Jayden let out a resigned sigh. Angie had been asking him to go with her every week since they'd started dating, but he'd always had an excuse. Now he couldn't think of any. "I guess I'll have to come this time. You win."

"Great, I'll pick you up at six."

Jayden stood and held Angie's hand as they walked out of

the café. Once outside, he turned and smiled at her. "I'll look forward to it."

She returned his smile, and stretching up, popped a quick kiss on his cheek. "And so will I."

JAYDEN RETURNED TO THE STORE, lost in thought. Jessica Morgan, pregnant? Unbelievable. He shook his head and returned to the shelves he'd left half stocked. The Morgan girls were known as good girls around town. This was going to make tongues wag. Good girls didn't get pregnant, did they? She probably wouldn't go to Bible Study tomorrow night. Just as well—he wouldn't know what to say to her.

CHAPTER 2

$\mathscr{B}$ethany Morgan adjusted her husband's collar the following morning as he prepared to leave for the staff meeting. "Are you sure you want to do this, Robert?"

Robert placed his hands on her shoulders and gazed down at her. "No, Beth, I don't want to, but it's the right thing to do."

She drew in a breath and sighed. "I know. I just wish this wasn't happening; I can already hear the gossip that will go round town."

Robert drew her into his arms and kissed the top of her head. "It's going to be all right, Beth. We'll weather this storm. I agree it'd be better if it hadn't happened, but it has, and there's nothing we can do about it."

Tears pricked Bethany's eyes. Robert was right, there was nothing they could do about it. Their daughter was pregnant, and abortion was out of the question. They just had to face the music and be strong for Jessica's sake. "I'll be praying for you."

He released her from his embrace and held her at arm's length. "I know you will. Thank you."

Bethany stood on the porch of their sprawling home and waved as he drove down the driveway. "God be with you, Robert."

"IS DAD REALLY TELLING EVERYONE TODAY?" Jessica sat at the kitchen table with her arms crossed and a sullen expression on her face. Her eyes, tinged with red, were fixed on Bethany. Beside her, Blake fiddled with his phone. Angie sat opposite, leaning back in her seat, her hands wrapped around a mug of hot chocolate, and fourteen-year-old Simon watched television in the family room to the side.

Bethany's heart went out to her daughter—Jessica's anger was totally understandable. Until a few days' ago, only two others knew her secret; Angela and Blake. After today, all of Hunters Hollow would know. Well, not quite, but that's what Jessica had said last night when Robert told her what he was planning, and she probably wasn't far from wrong.

Jessica slid further down in her seat. "I may as well be dead."

Bethany sighed. *Dear God, please help me.* She slipped into the seat beside Jessica and put her arm lightly on Jessica's shoulder. "It's not as bad as that, Jess. It's better this way, you know it is. Everyone would know about it soon, anyway. At least this way, people can see we're supporting you."

A lump formed in Bethany's throat. All night her heart had been heavy as she imagined what it might be like for them all in the days, weeks and months ahead. It was all too raw, too fresh, too vivid, but it was happening, and she and Robert had to be strong and support Jessica. They had to handle the embarrassment of having a pregnant teenage daughter, knowing people would judge them. But how much worse for Jess and Blake? If they hadn't been held in such high esteem by their peers and teachers, no one would have blinked an eye.

Tears streamed down Jessica's cheeks.

Bethany hugged her. "It'll be okay, sweet pea. We're here for you." She gazed over Jessica's head. Blake was still fiddling with his phone. Bethany bit her lip. She and Robert were more than happy to offer him a home until he went to college, but he hadn't seemed quite as contrite as they would have expected. They'd give him the benefit of the doubt for now—he was most likely still trying to come to terms with it all himself, but they hoped he'd soon understand the enormity of the situation.

Blake must have felt her eyes on him, as he put his phone down and straightened. When she released her hold on Jessica, he took Jessica's hand. Jessica turned and leaned against him.

Bethany stood and rubbed her hands. "Okay, we've spent enough time talking, we need to get some jobs done."

Three pairs of eyes stared at her.

"Don't look at me like that. Being busy will help pass the time." She glanced round the table. "Or you can go and clean out the cow shed if you'd prefer."

"Mom…" Angie rolled her eyes. "You win. Tell us what you want us to do."

FOR THE REST of the day, Bethany kept her three children and Blake busy with jobs. Music she normally wouldn't listen to blared through the house, but at least it was Christian music, or so they said. She couldn't tell. *Teenagers.* The only reprieve was when Angie sat at the piano and practiced her exam pieces.

The day passed and Robert finally arrived home around four o'clock. Bethany waited outside on the porch as he lumbered towards her. He gave her a tired smile and wrapped his arms around her. They remained in silence for several moments. Inside, music still sounded from the upstairs' rooms, but outside, the sounds of the ranch filled her ears. Robert's brother, John, and his wife, Mary, lived nearby. John looked after the ranch which had been in the family for generations. He must be out in the fields, as a tractor rumbled in the distance. Fall had come early, and they'd need to harvest all the hay they could before the first snow fell.

She inhaled slowly. She'd stay in Robert's arms all day if she could, cocooned from the world and all its problems, but that wasn't the way to deal with things. She slowly pulled away and lifted her eyes. "How did it go?"

He held her gaze. "Amazingly well. They appreciated me being upfront, but there's no saying what the students will think when they find out."

"Oh Robert, how's she going to cope?" She gazed into her husband's clear blue eyes, searching for an answer.

"She'll be fine, don't you worry. She's stronger than you think."

"But it's going to be so hard for her."

Robert ran his hand lightly down her cheek. "It's not ideal, but it's not the end of the world. Everyone makes mistakes, just hers is obvious. Or soon will be."

"In the olden days she would have been sent off to a home for unwed mothers."

"I guess she would have." Robert placed his arm on her shoulder as they walked slowly towards the front door. He paused and faced her. "I also dropped in at the church on the way home and told Graham. Thought he should know, with Bible Study on tonight. Word might already have gotten out."

Bethany sighed. "What are they all going to think?"

"It could happen to anyone, Beth."

"But I feel I've failed her. It shouldn't have happened."

"Don't start saying that." Robert tilted her chin upwards as he gazed into her eyes. "You've been the best mother a girl could ask for. We'll stand by her and support her, regardless of what everyone thinks."

Bethany nodded, but tears stung her eyes. She swallowed hard, and sucked in a breath. "How can you be so calm?"

He shrugged. "We can't change what's happened, and it's no use beating ourselves or Jess up about it. Besides," he wiped her tears with a tissue, "you know what this means, don't you?"

Bethany shook her head. "No... what?"

"You're going to be a grandmother."

Bethany inhaled slowly as a small grin formed on her face. Robert was right. Jess was carrying a baby, a real little person; their grandchild, and right or wrong, they'd support and love her, regardless.

Jayden raced home from work on his bike, threw a frozen meal into the microwave, and quickly showered and dressed while it heated. He was eating the last bite when a car horn sounded. He peered out the window. Angie's car was parked just outside the apartment block. He gulped down his soda, picked up the Bible Angie had given him a week ago, and ran down the steps. Before opening the main door, he paused and steadied his breathing, not wanting to appear over eager.

He sauntered up to her car, a small Ford Focus she shared with Jess, and opened the passenger door. "Hey Angie. Thanks for picking me up."

Her whole face beamed. She really was the most beautiful girl.

"No problem. I'm glad you're coming."

If only they were going somewhere other than Bible Study, but at least he'd be with her. He could survive a Bible Study if Angie was beside him. "You didn't give me much choice." He flashed her a cheeky grin.

She let out a small chuckle before starting the engine.

"I guess Jessica and Blake aren't coming tonight?"

The smile slid off her face as she put the car into gear. "No. Dad went through with it, so news will start spreading now." She glanced at him before pulling away from the curb. "Jess didn't want to face everyone just yet."

Jayden rubbed his forehead. "If some of them know already, you might get asked about it tonight. Are you ready for that?"

"Since when have you been so sensitive?" Angie flashed him a playful smile before her expression changed. "But yes, I had thought about that. Not sure it would have spread that quickly, but if it has, I'll deal with it. They'll know soon enough anyway. Dad told Pastor Graham this afternoon, so he knows already."

"Wow." Jayden drew a breath and faced the front. As he did,

he thought he saw Mom driving the other way. He quickly turned his head, but the car disappeared around a corner. Maybe it wasn't her. Either way, he should try to see her sometime soon, although since he'd moved out of the cottage she shared with Buck, she'd been avoiding him. He really didn't know what to feel about her anymore. Some days he couldn't care less, other days he felt sorry for her. Today, well, he really didn't know.

Angie slowed down and pulled into the parking lot of the Hunters Hollow Gospel Church. After switching off the engine, she turned and faced him, touching his wrist lightly. "They're a nice bunch, Jayden. You'll be fine."

He'd recognized a few of the young people he'd met at church last Sunday from when he went to school, but no one he really knew. But they seemed all right. Better than Roger and his old group from Austin. "I'll be okay."

"All right, then, let's go."

Angie took his hand as they strolled towards the church hall. It actually felt kind of good, almost normal. But his life was anything but normal. Would he fit in? Would they accept him?

CHAPTER 3

*L*aughter and music flowed from the church's meeting room as Jayden and Angela entered the building. Pausing outside the door, Jayden drew a steadying breath. Despite feeling nervous, in some ways he was interested to see what it was all about. Angie had told him they were starting a series entitled '*How can you know if God exists?*' After his experience in that church on Christmas Eve, where he thought he'd heard from God, this was a topic that actually interested him. Was God real, or was He just a figment of everyone's imagination?

"You okay?" Angie smiled as she squeezed his hand.

He nodded. "Yep. And you?"

"Yes, I'm good. Let's go."

She led him into a room where about twenty young people stood around talking and laughing in small groups, but his attention was drawn to the three boys sitting at the far end. One had a guitar strapped around his shoulder, another perched in front of a keyboard, and the third boy sat behind a set of drums.

"Join them if you want. There's a spare guitar over there." Angie nodded towards the wall nearest them.

"I don't know what they're playing."

She shook her head and laughed. "Let me introduce you, at least."

"If you have to."

She dragged him to where the boys were sitting. "Hey Gareth, this is Jayden." Gareth was the guitar player, and with his friendly face, he reminded Jayden a little of Neil. "Jayden plays the guitar really well."

"Yeah? Grab this one and join us." Gareth leaned over and picked up the spare guitar and handed it to him. "It's Johnno's, but he's away."

"Cool, as long as you don't mind." A grin grew on Jayden's face as he took the guitar and sat beside Gareth.

"What do you normally play?"

Jayden stiffened. Would Gareth think he was boasting if he told him he played a Gibson? He let out a breath. Best to play it safe. "Just an acoustic."

"Cool. Hey, this is Matt on the keyboard, and Dave on the drums."

Jayden gave them both a quick nod. The boys, who seemed a little older than him, leaned forward and held out their hands. Jayden shook both in turn.

"We're just having a bit of a jam. Wanna follow along?"

"Yeah." Jayden settled himself onto the chair and tested the guitar, a basic acoustic that sounded tinny and hollow compared to his, but it didn't matter. It'd been too long since he'd played with someone else. As the boys began to play, he followed along. He had no idea what they were playing, but it sounded pretty cool, just a lot lighter than he was used to.

Angie stood nearby, her face angled so she could see him. She was talking with an older man who was balding on top. Jayden recognized him as the pastor. There was only one thing they'd be talking about. *Jessica.*

Before long, a few of the young people stopped talking and pulled up chairs in front of the music team and began singing along. Jayden hadn't been aware that they'd been playing songs that had words to them. He thought they were just jamming, which was what he and Neil had always done. It was kind of strange, but also kind of cool.

The pastor left Angie and walked to the front. The band stopped playing at the end of the song, and those who'd still been talking finished their conversations and pulled up chairs in a semi-circle.

Angie sat on a seat beside Jayden and slipped her hand into his, flashing him a warm smile.

The pastor cleared his voice. "Well, hello everyone. Great to see you all here tonight. For those who are new, I'm Pastor Graham Simpson, and tonight we're starting a series entitled *'How can you know if God exists?'* But first, let's open in prayer."

Angie squeezed Jayden's hand. He caught her eye again before bowing his head. It seemed a little strange to be sitting here holding his girlfriend's hand when they were about to pray, but if she was okay with it, well, he guessed it must be all right, and tried to focus on the prayer.

"Dear God, we pray You'll be with us as we study Your word, and we ask that You'll open our hearts and minds as we seek to know the truth about You and how we can be sure that You actually are real in a world that believes You're not. Bless our time together, Lord God. Amen."

Pastor Graham looked up, his gaze traveling around the group. "I'd like to start this series by reading from Romans chapter 1, verse 20. You can read along or just listen." He flicked to the verse in his Bible and then began. "'*For since the creation of the world, God's invisible qualities—His eternal power and divine nature—have been clearly seen, being understood from what has been made, so that people are without excuse.'*

"Over the next few weeks, we're going to look into this passage and others more deeply, but before we do, here are the questions we're going to investigate. This verse claims that God's eternal power and divine nature are clearly visible in creation, but is there any way of finding out how it all came into being, or do we just have to take a giant leap of faith and believe that God created it because He said He did? If there is evidence, why don't more people believe in Him, or if they do, why do so many live like they don't? Assuming there is proof that God exists, what does it take to turn someone from non-belief in God to belief?

"These are huge questions. Questions that as young people I'm sure you've asked yourselves many a time." He shrugged. "Or maybe not. I hope that by the time we reach the end of the series, those of you who've been brought up in Christian homes and in the church, and have made a commitment to live for Jesus, will have a better understanding of *why* you believe, because it's far too easy just to accept what you've been told without really knowing why you do. And for those who haven't made a commitment yet but are searching for the truth, I hope and pray that you'll find what you're looking for, and that once you do, you'll be willing to commit your life to God, knowing that your belief isn't just a leap of faith, but is backed with solid proof."

The pastor's gaze traveled around the group again. "Your generation is very fortunate because there's more verification for the truth now than at any previous time in history, and I'm excited to be doing this study with you."

Jayden's mind raced. This was so different from what he'd expected. He'd never really thought there was any proof for God's existence, so if there was, he was interested in finding out about it. Strange, really, because even less than a year ago, he couldn't have cared less about God, but something had been stirring inside him, and he wanted to know what it was, but he wasn't about to jump blindly into believing.

Angie nudged him. Everyone was opening their study guides.

He opened his to Chapter One: *'Is Truth Absolute or Relative?'* He was ready for this. He'd study the information and then make a decision.

At the end of the study, the band was asked to play a few songs. Gareth nodded to him to join them.

He stiffened. It was one thing playing earlier when they were only jamming, but now everyone would see him.

Angie leaned closer and squeezed his arm. "Go on, you'll be fine."

He took a breath and followed Gareth to the front. He picked up the spare guitar and took the lead from the others, and before long he was enjoying playing songs that although weren't familiar, held words that spoke of God's love and grace, whatever that was.

After the singing, they entered into a prayer time. Jayden closed his eyes and listened. He'd never heard such heartfelt prayers before, even back home at Dad and Tessa's church. But then, he hadn't gone to the youth group meetings. And he wouldn't have listened even if he had. But these kids seemed genuine, but maybe it was just emotion, and he didn't want to get caught up in that, because what if that's all it was? He'd heard about that happening to people. No, it had to be real and true if he was going to believe and follow. He'd do lots of study before making up his mind.

At the end of the prayer time, Gareth placed his guitar into its case. Jayden followed suit.

"Coming to supper?" Gareth asked.

Jayden glanced at Angie, but she was talking with another girl. He shrugged. "Guess so. I'll see what Angie says."

"She normally comes."

"Guess we'll be coming, then." Jayden's secret hopes of spending time just with Angie flew out the window, but maybe it was time he made some new friends, and Gareth seemed like a cool dude.

The ice-cream parlor was about a mile away, and during the short drive there, Angie asked Jayden what he thought of the study.

"Not what I expected, but I'm glad I went."

Angie turned her head and gave him a smile. "I am too, Jayden."

"That pastor seems pretty smart."

"Yeah, he is. We all like him a lot."

"So what did he say about Jess?"

The smile slipped from Angie's face.

"Sorry, I shouldn't have brought it up."

"No, it's okay. I'd just forgotten about it for a moment." She glanced at him as she turned a corner. "He just asked how I was handling it. Said he was surprised, but that he'd support her and us in whatever way he could."

Jayden shifted in his seat. "It's going to be tough on her, isn't it?"

Angie nodded, a tear rolling down her cheek. "Sorry. Just every time I think about it, I get sad for her, and I try to think what it'd be like to be in her situation." Angie wiped her cheek with her hand before changing down a gear and pulling up outside the ice-cream parlor. "Here we are. No more talk of Jess, okay? I don't want to cry in front of everyone."

"Sorry. I won't bring it up again." He leaned over and popped a kiss on her cheek.

"Thanks." She gave him a watery smile and dabbed her eyes again before opening the door.

He draped his arm lightly across her shoulder as they entered the parlor.

Gareth called them over and introduced Jayden to his girl-friend, Rachel, the girl Angie had been talking to at the end of the study.

"Haven't I seen you at the grocery store?" Gareth asked as he handed out menus.

"Yeah, I work there." Jayden lifted his chin. "Just until I find something better."

"You don't go to school?"

Here we go... "No, I had to leave." Jayden picked up his menu. "Maybe one day I'll go back."

Angie leaned into him. "Leave Jayden alone, Gareth."

Gareth held his hands up. "I was just being polite."

"I know. Anyway, you two played well together tonight."

Jayden breathed a sigh of relief. He didn't want Gareth or any of the others to know about his mother and why he'd left both home and school. Maybe he should make up some kind of story to tell them. But as soon as that thought popped into his head, he decided it would be a bad move. He already had too many lies in his life, like lying to Angie about his age. One day he'd have to confess to her that he was only turning sixteen, not seventeen, like he'd told her he was. But not yet.

"Yeah, you should come to my house one day and we can jam."

Jayden smiled. "I'd like that, thanks."

A short while later, after they'd eaten their ice-creams and sundaes, Angie dropped him back to his apartment. He sat with his hand resting on the door handle. He didn't want to get out. Angie would be going back home to a family who loved her. He'd be going back to a cold, empty apartment. He took his hand from the handle and slipped it behind her neck, pulling her close. He ran his hand through her hair. Soft, silky, bouncy hair. His heart beat faster. He wanted to kiss her so much. He lifted her head slowly until her lips were so close he could almost taste them. He lowered his head until their lips touched. Cradling her head in his hands, he pressed his lips harder. How he'd love to kiss her properly. His chest heaved.

She pulled away. Her face was flushed. She held a hand to

his cheek. "I'm sorry, Jayden. I can't do this." Her voice was soft, breathless.

His heart plummeted. He slowly straightened, drawing a deep breath to steady himself. He'd acted rashly. This was how Jessica had gotten into trouble. He'd lose Angie if he wasn't careful, and no way did he want that to happen.

He squeezed her hand. "I'm sorry, Ange. I got carried away. I didn't think."

"It's okay. I shouldn't have encouraged you."

Their eyes met and his heart pounded. How would he find the strength not to kiss her like that again? But it was wrong, and somehow he'd have to.

"You're so beautiful, Ange, I just wanted to hold you."

"Oh Jayden, don't be silly." She let out a small chuckle before her expression sobered. "But seriously, as much as I want to kiss you too, we need to do this right. I want to do things God's way, and I don't think I could trust myself if we got too close. Know what I mean?"

Unfortunately he did. "You take this God thing seriously, don't you?"

She nodded as she relaxed in her seat, inspecting her fingernails before she looked up. "I gave my heart to Jesus when I was ten, and I try to live my life as He'd want me to. It's not always easy. Like now." She rolled her eyes and let out another small chuckle. "But He gives me strength, even though I often let him down."

"I'd have thought you'd only date a Christian, then. Not someone like me."

She hung her head. "Mom and Dad talked to me about that. They told me to be careful, but left it up to me to decide whether I should go out with you or not." She paused for a second before raising her head and meeting his gaze. "I prayed about it, and I believe God's working in your heart, so I'm comfortable with our relationship."

Jayden pressed his lips together. Would Angie pressure him to become a Christian? He didn't like being manipulated. He'd had enough of that with Mom. "Maybe we just need to be friends for now, then."

Angie's face fell. "Don't be like that. You asked."

Jayden sighed. He didn't want to be 'just friends' anyway. What was he thinking?

"I really like you, and I want to be your girlfriend, but we can't kiss like that. Okay?"

Jayden nodded reluctantly. If that's what she wanted, that's what he'd have to do. *Somehow.* He smiled at her and squeezed her hand. "Okay."

"How about we pray before I go?"

His eyes widened. He'd do almost anything to make her happy. *But pray?* He drew a breath and shrugged. "Okay."

Angie took his hand and bowed her head. Her voice was so sweet. "Dear Heavenly Father, thank You for Your love, and for bringing Jayden into my life. I pray that You'll reveal Yourself to him over the next few weeks and months, and that he might come to know Your peace and love in his life, and that You'll wipe away all the hurts he's had with his family. And please bless our relationship. Help us to keep it pure and honorable in Your sight, dear Lord, even though it might be difficult at times. And Lord, please be with Jess and give her strength." Angie's voice caught. "Let her feel Your loving arms around her, dear Lord, and bless the little baby she's carrying. In Jesus' name, Amen."

Something stirred deep inside Jayden. But was it just emotion, or was it God?

JAYDEN KNEW he'd have trouble sleeping. The apartment was so quiet, and to be honest, he was lonely. After Angie left, he'd picked up his guitar and started strumming some of the music they'd played at the study, even though he couldn't remember all the words. After a short while, he put the guitar down and slumped back onto his bed. A myriad of thoughts whirled in his head. Angie, Jess, Mom, Dad, Tessa. *And God.* He let out a resigned sigh and sat up. He wasn't going to sleep any time soon, so he pulled the Bible and study guide off the bedside table. He may as well do some study. Opening the guide, he began reading through the notes again....*Truth has to be backed up by fact, it can't just be opinion. Nobody can invent truth, it gets discovered. It doesn't matter how genuinely someone believes something, if it's true, it's true, if it's false, it's false. Something can't be true for one person and false for another. Either Santa Claus is real, or he's not, despite what thousands of parents tell their children each Christmas. And God's either real, or he's not.* Jayden closed his book and leaned back against his pillow and yawned. *So why do so many people disagree?* He yawned again. That would have to wait until tomorrow night. He drifted off to sleep with images of Angie floating through his mind.

CHAPTER 4

*B*risbane, Australia

TESSA ALWAYS KNEW that Jayden's sixteenth birthday would be a difficult day for her and Ben, even though since returning from their mission trip to Ecuador, Ben had been more relaxed, and even confident that Jayden would one day come home.

Only last week they'd received another letter from him, and in it he'd told them he had a girlfriend. *A girlfriend!* How bitter sweet, not being part of such a major milestone in his life, but at least knowing he had someone special in his life gave them some comfort.

Tessa woke that morning and slipped out of bed quietly so as not to disturb Ben. Five months into her pregnancy, she was unable to stay in bed much past six o'clock. She threw on her robe, opened the door carefully, and tip-toed down the stairs. All her efforts at being quiet were ruined when Bindy and Sparky eyed her—their yaps were enough to waken the whole neighbourhood. "Shh… you'll wake Ben up." She bent down and gave them a pat before heading to the bathroom. When she came back out, both dogs sat in front of the door with eager faces and tails wagging. How could she deny them? She quickly changed into the light blue track suit she kept downstairs, put on her Nikes, and grabbed the dogs' leads. They followed her eagerly into the backyard where she clipped their leads onto their collars before slipping through the side gate.

The pale colours of dawn filled the sky, and the day promised to be a good one. Not a breath of breeze touched her as the dogs dragged her down the tree-lined street leading to the park and to the river. The aroma of freshly brewed coffee wafted in the air, tempting Tessa to stop as she approached the corner café where, despite the chill of the morning, the outdoor tables were filled with early morning walkers and cyclists enjoying a cup of the café's highly reputed coffee. Tessa glanced down at her two canine companions. They wouldn't be happy if she stopped. Besides, Ben would be up soon, and she needed to get back. No, coffee would have to wait.

She did a quick lap, just enough to satisfy the dogs, and then headed back home. Ben was in the kitchen getting the breakfast things out when she returned. She stretched up and placed a kiss on his cheek.

He leaned back against the kitchen bench and pulled her close, slipping his arms around her waist.

She rested her head on his chest before pulling back and gazing into his eyes, which were heavier and darker than normal. She touched his cheek. "We'll get through today. I know we will."

His chest expanded as he inhaled slowly. "You're always so positive." A wistful smile grew on his face. "Yes, we'll get through the day, but it'd be better if he was here."

"I know. But we have hope, and we need to be thankful for that." Tessa smiled into his eyes. "Why don't you write him another letter? At least that way it'll be like you're talking with him."

"Mmm, I might just do that." He tilted his head. "So what are we doing today?"

"Oh, I don't know… maybe we could go back to bed for a while?"

Ben raised an eyebrow, a playful grin forming on his face. "Great idea." He leaned down and kissed her gently before taking her hand and leading her upstairs.

SOMETIME LATER, Tessa woke to flutterings in her tummy. All her concerns about miscarrying again had been put to rest some time ago, and now, towards the end of her second trimester, their baby was alive and well. She wriggled up and leaned against the pillows. Beside her, Ben stirred. She reached out and gently placed his hand on her stomach.

He opened his eyes and smiled as he snuggled closer. "I think I could stay here all day."

Tessa laughed. "We could, but no." She straightened and glanced at the clock. "We promised to help at the working bee, and we're going to be late if we don't hurry."

Ben yawned. "Do we have to go?"

"We promised."

He let out a resigned sigh. "Best get ready, then." He leaned up and kissed her lips as he ran his hand down her cheek. "I love you, Tess. Thank you for being here for me."

"Where else would I be?" She laughed.

"Oh, I don't know. Just saying!"

She shook her head, but warmth spread through her body as Ben pulled her close and kissed her again. After several seconds, she pulled away. "Okay. We need to get ready. We can grab breakfast on the way."

He smiled at her. "Sounds good."

THE WORKING bee at the Fellowship Bible Church was well under way by the time they arrived, but Ben and Tessa were warmly welcomed by Fraser Stanthorpe, the pastor, and their friends, Margaret and Harold, as well as all the others who were busy doing a variety of jobs around the place.

Ben was allocated the job of trimming the bushes at the front of the building with Scott and Rosy, a young couple who'd been attending the Bible Study group Ben was leading in their home. Tessa was given the job of window cleaning with Margaret.

"Good to see you here, Tessa." Margaret's warm smile lit up her face. "Harold and I have been praying for you both." She glanced towards the front of the building and lowered her voice. "How's Ben holding up today?"

Tessa inhaled slowly. "It's going to be a long day."

Margaret nodded. "Being here will do him good."

"Yes."

The working bee was due to finish at twelve o'clock. An idea formed in Tessa's mind as she cleaned windows beside Margaret, and when Ben came inside, she put her hand on his shoulder and whispered into his ear. He turned to face her and then nodded.

Tessa called everyone to attention. She cleared her throat as her gaze travelled around the group of about twenty people. "Ben and I would like to invite you all back to our place for lunch. It's Jayden's sixteenth birthday today, and even though he's not here, we'd like to celebrate it with our friends." Her voice choked and tears stung her eyes, but she pushed them back. She wasn't going to be sad. She took a deep breath and leaned into Ben.

"That's a very kind offer," Fraser said. "Tracy and I would love to come, thank you."

"And so would we," Margaret said, wiping her eyes as she reached for Harold's hand.

Most of the others also accepted, offering to bring food for the impromptu meal.

Tessa thought a simple barbecue would be the easiest, and she and Ben stopped at the supermarket on the way home and bought hamburger patties and bread rolls, as well as tomatoes, lettuce and beetroot. They had plenty of onions and cheese at home. Margaret offered to bring some cake for dessert, and a few others said they'd bring drinks.

Shortly after, when everyone arrived, Ben began cooking the hamburger patties and onions on the barbecue. Fraser, Harold, and Scott stood around the barbecue chatting and laughing. Tessa's heart warmed as she glanced through the kitchen window while she and Margaret buttered the bread rolls. *Thank you, God. This is just what Ben needs.*

"You really do have a lovely home, Tessa." Margaret glanced around the open-plan kitchen and living area that opened out onto the timber deck surrounded by a sub-tropical garden and a large in-ground pool.

"Thank you." Tessa gave her an appreciative smile. "We think it's a mansion after being in Ecuador, which it probably is, but we feel so much better about it now it's being used for God's work. We love having people over, and it's been great for Bible Study."

"I've heard good things about the study Ben's leading."

Tessa smiled. "Yes, he's doing a great job. Ecuador changed him so much." Her heart overflowed with gratitude as she gazed out at Ben. How much God had blessed them. The trip to Ecuador had been a turning point in their lives, no doubt about it. They'd both come back with a much stronger faith and understanding of what it meant to trust God, and they'd both learned to let things go. So many things that in the past would have upset them or caused them to worry, now seemed insignificant.

"And this was a great idea. Thank you."

"Our pleasure. It's great to have the house filled with friends. Especially today."

Margaret placed her hand lightly on Tessa's wrist. "He'll be back soon, I'm sure of it."

"Maybe, but now he's got a girlfriend..." Tessa raised a brow. "Who knows?"

"Don't give up hope, dear."

"We're not, it's just that it's hard being patient."

"Tell me about it!" Margaret let out a chuckle. "But when it finally happens, it's like all that lost time is forgotten. I'm sure it'll be the same for you as well."

"I hope so. I truly do."

LATER, after everyone had eaten, Margaret brought out a chocolate cake she'd picked up on her way from church. She lit sixteen candles, and placed the cake in front of Ben and Tessa. "Let's sing happy birthday to Jayden."

Tessa smiled at Margaret and then leaned into Ben. Her heart ached as they sang, and tears filled her eyes, but she was ever so glad they were surrounded by friends who understood their pain and were there to support them.

"Can we pray for Jayden?" Fraser's normally strong voice was quiet and full of compassion.

Tessa glanced up at Ben before nodding. "That would be great, thank you."

Fraser smiled and then cleared his throat. "Let's pray." He bowed his head. "Dear God, we thank You for this beautiful day, and for this beautiful family. We can't even begin to understand the heartache that Ben and Tessa are feeling, but You understand, dear Lord, and we pray that today as they celebrate Jayden's sixteenth birthday, that You'll comfort them and wrap Your arms around them. And we also pray for Jayden. We ask that You'll be with him, that You'll keep him safe, and that You'll keep knocking on the door of his heart, and we pray that one day soon he'll let You in. Bless the new little baby that's soon to be welcomed into this family, dear

CHAPTER 4 | 31

Lord, and may Your name continue to be glorified in this home. In Jesus' precious name, Amen."

Tessa sucked in a breath as she wiped her eyes. Fraser's prayer had acted as a balm to her soul. She raised her head and gazed around the group, thanking God for bringing each one of them into her life.

AFTER THEY'D ALL LEFT, Tessa flopped onto a sun-lounge, resting her head on a cushion. "I think I need a nap, Ben."

"I'm not surprised." Ben perched beside her and brushed his hand over her hair. "Thanks for organising that. It was great."

She took his other hand and held it. "Funny how spontaneous events are often better than overly planned ones."

"I'm beginning to learn that!" He chuckled as he lowered his face before placing a gentle kiss on her lips. "I'll go write that letter while you nap."

She smiled before stifling a yawn. "Great idea."

CHAPTER 5

While Tessa napped, Ben sat at his computer and stared at the screen. So many things he wanted to say to Jayden, but now he didn't know where to start. He spun around in his chair and gazed out at Tessa sleeping on the sun-lounge, cozily wrapped in a blanket. He drew in a deep breath and picked up Jayden's latest letter. He knew the contents by heart, but read it again anyway.

DEAR DAD AND TESSA,

You know I'm not that good at writing letters, so I'll keep this short. I'm doing okay. Work is all right, but it's a bit boring. I never thought I'd be stocking shelves for a job, but at least I get paid every week. The lady I work with keeps telling me I need to be studying. I will, one day. My biggest news is that I've got a girlfriend. Her name's Angie, and she's really nice. It was her parents who told me I should write to you. They're really cool. They live on a ranch, but Mr.

Morgan is a teacher at the high school. They also go to church, and I've been going with them for the past few weeks. I know you'll be happy about that. I don't see Mum very often, but she's not in a good way. I keep an eye out for her in case she needs me. How are Bindy and Sparky? I miss them. I'm not ready to talk yet, but I'm glad we can write to each other and that you're not mad at me.

Your son,
Jayden

BEN BLINKED BACK tears as he slowly folded the paper. *How did this happen, God? How did Jayden end up on the other side of the world?* He swallowed the lump in his throat and sucked in a deep breath before exhaling slowly. God was working in Jayden's heart, and at least they were communicating. He needed to be thankful for that. But it was still, oh so hard.

A flock of brightly coloured rainbow lorikeet parrots flew overhead and settled in the grevillea bush in the far corner of the yard and twittered, triggering memories of the camping trip they'd taken to the mountains. Such a fun weekend, although he hadn't wanted to go. He sighed heavily. *Will we ever to get to do that again?*

He turned back to his desk, but instead of typing, he pulled out a piece of paper and a pen. *God, please give me the words to write.*

Dear Jayden,

This is such a hard letter to write. Today is your sixteenth birthday, and Tessa and I are wondering what you're doing for it. We're guessing you'll be spending it with your girlfriend, and maybe her family. They sound really nice. Whatever you do, we hope you have a great day.

BEN RAN his hand through his hair. It wasn't right—Jayden should be spending his birthday with him and Tessa, not with another family. But he had to put that aside.

It's hard for us to imagine you with a girlfriend. You must have grown up so much, and we're proud of the way you're taking on such responsibility, but we can't pretend we're not sad that you still haven't come home. Know that whenever you do decide to come, you'll be welcomed with open arms. Bindy and Sparky will be so excited to see you too. They miss you terribly.

We would have liked to celebrate your birthday with you today, but as we couldn't, we celebrated it anyway. It's been a lovely day, even though the guest of honour was missing. We miss you, Jayden, and we look forward to the day when we'll see you again.

And yes, both Tessa and I were pleased to hear you've been to church. And we're happy you've found a family to spend time with. Maybe you could send a photograph with your next letter?

Until then, be assured of our love, which will never change, no matter where you are or what you do.

Dad

. . .

SIGHING, Ben placed his pen on the desk and folded the paper. One step at a time. It was all he could ask for, and he had to be content with that.

He hadn't heard Tessa come in, but her hand on his shoulder was warm and soft. He reached up and placed his hand on hers before spinning slowly around in his chair.

"Done?" Her voice still sounded sleepy, and her hair was messed up.

He pulled her gently onto his lap, blanket and all, slipping his arms around her waist. "Yes, it's done."

"Good." She leaned her head on his and wrapped her arms around his neck and shoulders.

Moments of silence passed between them. He closed his eyes. Tessa's love kept him going. He nuzzled her hair. So soft. And the smell... He breathed in her perfume as he kissed the curve of her neck. Her head rolled slowly. His pulse quickened. His kisses grew more urgent. He lifted his hand and tilted her face towards his. He opened his eyes and gazed into hers.

"We couldn't do this if Jayden was here." Tessa's eyes sparkled, her voice no more than a whisper.

"We'd better make the most of it, then." He pulled her closer until their lips met in a kiss that began gently, but grew in intensity, leaving them both breathless.

"WE'RE GOING TO BE LATE." Tessa threw off her blanket and stood. Her chest heaved. "You get distracted so easily these days."

Ben laughed. "What do you expect? We're here on our own, and you're so deliciously beautiful."

It was true. Not that she was so deliciously beautiful, he could say that if he wanted, but it was true that apart from their honeymoon, they'd never really been on their own. Even at the mission, people were always popping in at random times, but here, in their own home, it was almost like they were newlyweds.

"We told Mum and Dad we'd be there by six." Tessa glanced at her watch. "It's five-thirty now."

"We'd better hurry, then. Just one more kiss?" Ben cocked his head. His eyes were so soft and doey. She almost gave in.

"No. Come on, we need to get ready."

Ben blew out a breath and stuck his bottom lip out. "If we have to." He stood, but as he did, he grabbed her hand and pulled her close. "I do love you, Tess. With all my heart."

She smiled up at him. "I know. And I love you too."

He leaned down and placed a gentle kiss on her lips.

ELEANOR AND TELFORD stood outside the new Modern Australian restaurant Tessa had suggested trying after seeing it on one of her early morning walks with the dogs.

"Sorry we're late." Tessa gave her mother and father a hug and a kiss, while Ben greeted Eleanor with a kiss and Telford with a handshake.

"No problem, dear, we were just admiring the view. The

river always looks spectacular at night." Eleanor gave her a warm smile as she linked her arm through Tessa's. "And this place looks interesting. A little different to Bussey's."

Tessa chuckled. "You could say that. But it's well and truly time you and Dad tried something different."

"Not so sure about trying crocodile, though." Telford raised his bushy eyebrows as a look of mock terror appeared on his face.

"Oh Dad, be adventurous for once!" Tessa slapped him playfully on the back as they strolled towards the entrance of 'Bree's on the River'.

"It's so modern and fancy," Eleanor said as they stepped inside the door and waited to be seated. The restaurant was expansive, with an open-air feel to it. Perched on the edge of the river, the jogging path was the only separation between the restaurant and the waterway that was the life of the city. Tonight, a steady stream of couples strolled along the path, with the occasional cyclist weaving around them. On the river, the CityCat skimmed past, leaving a ripple of small waves in its wake. The gentle sound of water lapping the river's edge greeted them as they took their seats at their table on the outside alfresco deck.

"Glad I wore a jacket." Tessa shivered and rubbed her arms briskly as a light breeze came off the river.

"I'll ask them to light a heater," Ben said, calling a waiter over.

"That's better," Tessa said as their young, smart-looking waiter ignited the gas heater, sending an immediate blast of warmth her way.

"I have to admit this is lovely, Tessa." Her mother's gaze swept around the restaurant and along the river.

"Still don't know what was wrong with Bussey's." Her father folded his arms and wriggled in his seat.

"Dad. Stop it!"

He laughed. "I'm just teasing." His eyes crinkled at the edge as his face softened into a playful grin. "But I'm still not so sure about the menu."

"We can always have fish." Eleanor leaned against him and lifted her eyes.

Telford placed his arm around her shoulders and gave her a squeeze. "Yes, we could."

Tessa shook her head. One day she'd get them to try something different.

They placed their orders. Ben chose the Seared Kangaroo Fillet with fresh raspberries and char grilled spring onions. She chose the Smoked Duck Breast with potato gallet and glazed baby carrots. Her parents both chose the Fish of the Day, which was a Pan Fried Coral Trout with kipfler potatoes, broccolini and truss cherry tomatoes.

"I'm not sure about Coral Trout. Would have preferred Barramundi," her father said, the playful grin returning to his face.

Tessa glared at him before bursting out in laughter. "Whatever." Her smile quickly slipped from her face. The last time she'd heard that word it'd come out of Jayden's mouth when they were in New Zealand, the day before he disappeared. It was like it happened yesterday. Jayden stood in the doorway of their hotel room, engrossed in his phone, while Neil waited for him to leave for their snowboarding lesson with Eversley.

Jayden's attitude was so bad Ben had come close to hitting him. And then came the 'whatever' word. She released a slow breath. It wasn't what she wanted to remember tonight.

"Are you all right, dear?" Mum leaned forward and touched her wrist.

Tessa drew a slow breath and steadied herself before meeting her mother's gaze. "Yes, I just had a sudden flashback, that's all."

"Jayden?" her father asked.

She nodded.

"We wondered how you were both holding up," Mum said.

Ben slipped his arm around her shoulders and pulled her close. "We've survived." His deep voice was steady and controlled, but more subdued than normal. Yes, they'd survived, but only just. "Tessa organised an impromptu lunch at our house after the working bee. It helped."

"That's good to hear." Mum offered a soft smile. "I'm sure he'll be home soon."

"You sound just like Tessa." Ben shook his head as he let out a small chuckle. "I don't know how you can both be so confident."

"I guess we're just hopeful, that's all. Nobody really knows what's going to happen with him apart from God, but we can keep on praying, and asking God to keep working on him. I'm sure that one day he will come home. We just hope and pray it'll be sooner rather than later."

"Yes, but he's got a girlfriend now."

"A girlfriend?" Dad's eyebrows waggled.

"I told you, Telford. Don't you remember?" An expression holding a hint of frustration flashed across Mum's face.

"Can't say I do."

Tessa drew her eyebrows together and looked at her mother. *Is something wrong with Dad? He seems very forgetful of late.*

She averted her gaze, as if she didn't want to acknowledge Tessa's unspoken question.

"Yes, well, he's got a girlfriend." Ben shifted in his seat.

"A bit young for one of them, I'd say." Dad's eyebrows waggled again.

"Sounds like he's grown up a lot, Ben." Mum's voice was soft and warm. "We might not recognise him anymore."

Ben sighed. "I know. That's what worries us."

"We'll know him." Tessa squeezed his hand. "He'll just be older, that's all."

A waiter stopped by their table with drinks and a share platter for entrée. After he'd left, Telford held up his glass. "Let's drink to Jayden's sixteenth birthday."

Tessa clinked her glass with the other three, praying silently for Jayden as gratitude that at least Dad had remembered how old Jayden was swept over her.

CHAPTER 6

*a*s Jayden pushed his cart into the pet food aisle, he glanced towards the front of the store and caught his breath. Mom stood near the register, talking with Charmian. His pulse quickened as he paused and peered down the aisle. Had Mom remembered his birthday?

He left the cart and strolled as casually as he could to the front.

Charmian looked up and called him over, extending her arm.

Mom lowered her gaze to the floor as he approached.

"Hey Mom. How are you doing?" Jayden sidled up to her and placed his hand lightly on her shoulder. His hand recoiled at the bones protruding through her thin shirt.

She raised her head slowly and gave him a weak smile, not the flashy over-the-top smile she used to give him, instead, one that seemed like it was almost too much effort. "I'm doing all right, Jay. Good to see you." Her eyes lit up for a second before she lowered them again and reached inside her purse.

Jayden held his breath. *Maybe she's remembered.*

But instead of pulling out a gift, she pulled out a tissue. His shoulders sagged. Why wasn't he surprised?

"Take a break if you'd like," Charmian said, touching his wrist lightly.

"Thanks." He gave Charmian a grateful smile, and then turned his gaze to Mom. "Would you like to have breakfast?"

Her eyes lit up. "That would be lovely."

"No problem. Let's go."

As he placed his arm lightly around her shoulders and led her out of the store, he glanced at Charmian and gave her a backwards wave.

"So how are you really doing?" Jayden asked as they sat at a table towards the back of the café he often frequented with Angie. He steadied his gaze as he tried hard not to let his disappointment show. How could his own mother have forgotten his sixteenth birthday? So much for all her promises.

"I'm okay. Buck's still looking after me."

Jayden shook his head. He knew exactly what that meant. He'd seen her latest lot of bruises, even though she'd obviously tried to cover them.

"Why don't you leave him? I can make room for you at my place."

"Oh Jay, if only I could."

Jayden gritted his teeth. "I don't see why it's so hard."

Her eyes narrowed. "You don't understand."

Jayden raised an eyebrow. "Obviously not." He shook his head and let out a heavy sigh. "You'd better eat before it gets cold." He nodded towards her sausage and egg sandwich. "Looks like you could do with some good food."

She shrugged as she lifted the sandwich and took a bite.

Jayden picked at his pancakes, but his appetite had disappeared the moment Mom turned up.

WHEN HE RETURNED to the store a short while later, Charmian stepped away from the register and gave him a bear hug. "You did the right thing leaving her. She would have pulled you down with her if you'd stayed."

Jayden's eyes misted over as a heavy weight settled on his heart. He gulped, wiping his eyes quickly. "I know. But it's still hard. I just wish she'd leave him." He struggled to hold himself together.

"We all do. Trust me." Charmian gave him another hug before reaching down below the register. She pulled out a small package and with a warm smile on her face, gave it to him. "Happy seventeenth birthday, Jayden. It's not much, but I hope you like it. The boys helped me choose it."

Jayden's eyes widened. "How did you know?"

"You wrote your date of birth on the application when you started here."

"Oh." The day and month were correct, but the year... he'd have to come clean one day. "Thank you." He smiled gratefully and took the parcel.

"The boys have been asking when you're going to come around." She chuckled. "I told them you had a girlfriend now, so you might not be too interested in seeing them anymore."

"That's not true. I'd love to see them."

"Well, feel free to come over whenever you want. I guess you'll be seeing Angela tonight?"

Jayden nodded. "Yes, I'm going there right after work today."

"They're good people, the Morgan's." Her expression grew serious, and she stepped closer. "I heard about the other daughter. Is it true what they're saying?"

Jayden sucked in a breath. *Here we go*. All week he'd been getting sly looks from a number of customers, although none had actually said anything to him directly. But they knew about Jess being pregnant, no doubt about it. He'd have to tell her. "Yes, it's true. Jess is pregnant."

Charmian shook her head and tutted. "The poor girl. How's she coping?"

Jayden shrugged. "Angie says she's doing okay. She's back at school."

Charmian raised an eyebrow. "Where you should be, young man."

He let out a resigned sigh. "I know. I'll go back one day."

An elderly woman, one of their regular customers, hobbled into the store.

Charmian smiled and waved to the woman, who, despite having to walk with a cane, was always well dressed and wore a full face of make-up. "Good morning, Mrs. Johnson."

"Good morning, dear." Mrs. Johnson's kind face broke into a wrinkly smile.

"I'd better get on." Jayden lifted his package and smiled at Charmian. "Thanks for this."

"My pleasure. Have a great day."

He wandered back to the boxes of dog food and began

stocking again. If only Mom was like Charmian. But she wasn't, and he just had to accept it. At least Dad and Tessa hadn't forgotten his birthday. A parcel had turned up yesterday with a framed photo of Bindy and Sparky, along with a birthday card. He'd almost been tempted to jump on a plane and go home. He would have, if it hadn't been for Angie.

The rest of the morning, he checked the time almost every ten minutes or so. Four hours had never seemed so long. Twelve o'clock finally came around and he was able to leave. He didn't know why they'd even bothered opening. Apart from Mrs. Johnson, they'd only had two other customers. Seemed everyone was at the Saturday markets this week.

Jayden grabbed his bag and gift from the lunch room and bid goodbye to Charmian, who was closing off the register. "See you Monday, and thanks again." He held up the gift and gave her a wave.

As he stepped outside into the clean, fresh air, he looked expectantly left, then right. Angie hadn't said she'd pick him up, but he hoped she would. He could ride his bike out to the ranch, but it'd better if he went with Angie. His heart skipped a beat every time he thought of her, but now she was back at school, he could only see her on weekends and on Wednesday nights at Bible Study. If he was at school, he'd see her every day, but he couldn't afford to quit his job, so that wasn't going to happen.

He'd just started walking when a car horn sounded. He turned and smiled as Angie's silver Ford Focus pulled up beside him. She stretched across to the passenger side and opened the door.

"Hey Jayden, thought I might catch you. Happy birthday!"

He jumped into the car. "Thanks. Do I get a birthday kiss?" He leaned the side of his head towards her and waited. With proper kissing off limits, they'd agreed a cheek kiss would be okay, but it was killing him. She was wearing the perfume he'd bought to celebrate their one-month anniversary. Charmian had suggested it. Not that she knew what perfume girls liked because she had all boys, but he didn't have a clue. Seemed Angie liked it though, so it must have been all right. At least she was wearing it. But the smell of it only made him want to hold her. He held his head still, waiting. Her finger touched his chin. His heart thumped as she slowly turned his face around until their eyes met. Her lips were so close. She leaned closer until their lips brushed. Her kiss was soft and tender.

"Just because it's your birthday." Her eyes sparkled, and then she smiled. Not just an ordinary smile, but one that lit up her face, making him want to pull her close and hold her tight. His hands began to sweat. He was falling in love. His heart beat faster. How was he going to keep their agreement?

She laughed. "What's with you? Come on, let's get out of here." She clicked her seatbelt on, put the car into gear and pulled out onto the road. All the way back to her place she chatted, but all he could think about was how much he loved her.

When they pulled into the long driveway that led up to the house, Angie stopped the car and looked at him. "You've hardly said a word. Is something wrong?"

He looked down and fiddled with his hands. He couldn't tell her he loved her. Not yet. What if she laughed at him? He lifted his head and looked into her eyes. "Nothing's wrong. Just thinking, that's all."

"Are you sad?"

"Kind of. I saw Mom today. She didn't remember it was my birthday."

"You poor thing." Angie's face softened.

"But Charmian gave me a present." Jayden opened his bag and pulled it out. "Guess I should open it."

"Go on then."

He returned it to the bag. "Nuh, I'll do it later."

"Okay." Angie's eyes lit up as another huge smile grew on her face. "You'll never guess what I've got you."

"Give me a clue?"

She laughed. "No, you can guess." She eased off the clutch and inched the car up the deeply rutted gravel driveway. Within minutes they were pulling into the garage alongside Mr. Morgan's white SUV, making her Ford Focus look even tinier than it was. Jayden still hadn't guessed what his present was.

MRS. MORGAN WAS PULLING a pizza out of the oven as they entered the kitchen a few moments later.

"Smells great, Mom." Angie gave her mom a peck on the cheek and swung her bag off her shoulder.

"Thanks sweetie." Bethany Morgan placed the pizza on a trivet, wiped her hands on her apron before taking it off, and extended her arms to Jayden. "And happy birthday, Jayden."

Her smile was the same as Angie's, warm and friendly, and apart from Angie, and maybe Charmian, Mrs. Morgan was the only other person Jayden was happy to hug. He always felt welcome here in her kitchen, the hub of the sprawling house where the whole family gathered, but today, no one else was about, although music filtered down from somewhere upstairs.

Jayden stepped into her embrace and returned her hug. "Thank you."

"My pleasure. And you're just in time for lunch. Angela, can you call the others?"

"Sure." Angie disappeared upstairs, leaving Jayden alone with Mrs. Morgan.

He stood awkwardly, not really knowing what to do. Angie was always with him, but Mrs. Morgan began chatting just like Angie did, and told him to pull up a stool and asked if he'd like a drink, and then asked how work was this morning, and before he realized it, he was telling her about Mom's visit to the store.

"Sounds like she's in a bad way. It's a sad situation, from what I hear."

He drew a breath and wrapped his hands around his glass of soda, struggling to control the sudden wave of sadness that hit him. All of a sudden he had the urge to confide about how he was feeling, but the sound of voices coming closer stopped him. Another time, maybe.

"Yeah, she's pretty messed up."

"We pray for her every day, just like we pray for you. No situation is so bad that God can't fix it." Mrs. Morgan gave him another smile that tugged at his heart. How could she do this in just a matter of minutes? He drew in a steadying breath and finished his drink, just as Angie, Jess and Simon entered the kitchen.

"Where's your father?" Mrs. Morgan asked of no one in particular.

"He's coming." Angie pulled out a stool and sat beside Jayden.

"We know what that means." Mrs. Morgan rolled her eyes and gave a small chuckle.

"No, he said he'd be right down."

"And here I am." Mr. Morgan strolled in and placed his hands on his wife's shoulders as she stood in front of the kitchen counter slicing a pizza. "Let me do that, Beth. It smells great."

Mrs. Morgan stood aside, allowing him to take over while she tossed the salad.

"I believe birthday wishes are in order, Jayden." Mr. Morgan glanced up and looked towards him. "Any plans for the day?"

Jayden glanced at Angie. "We were thinking of going for a ride."

"If that's okay?" Angie stole a cherry tomato from the salad and popped it into her mouth.

"Can I come?" Simon asked, looking up from his iPad, sounding quite eager.

Angie glared at him.

"Great idea," Mr. Morgan replied. "Maybe you'd like to go too, Jess?"

Jessica shook her head violently as she slapped her hand over her mouth. She slid off the stool and raced out of the room.

Jayden's stomach churned at the sound of her vomiting.

"She's having a rough time of it, isn't she?" Mr. Morgan glanced towards the downstairs bathroom before turning his attention to the next pizza.

"Yes, poor dear," Mrs. Morgan paused, drawing a breath, "but going for a ride might do her good."

Jayden managed another quick sideways glance at Angie. She gave a small shrug as their eyes met briefly. They were going to be chaperoned, like it or not.

CHAPTER 7

"*L*unch was great, thank you, Mrs. Morgan."

"My pleasure, Jayden. Glad you enjoyed it." She had begun collecting the dirty plates off the outdoor table and was about to collect his.

His eye was on the last remaining slice of meat lover's pizza, but he held back, not wanting to appear rude in front of Angie's family. Besides, he'd already had more than Simon, and that was saying something. Angie's fourteen-year-old brother certainly had a good appetite for a small dude.

"Go on, have it." Mr. Morgan chuckled. "It's your birthday, after all."

Jayden looked up, his eyes widening. "Really?"

"Yes, go for it."

"Thank you." Jayden reached for the slice and popped it onto his plate, but Simon's eyes were on him. Jayden let out a small sigh. He'd have to share it. He lifted his gaze and looked at Simon. "Want half?"

"Yes please." Simon straightened and watched eagerly as Jayden cut it in half.

Mrs. Morgan angled her head and glared at him. "Simon!"

"He offered." Simon's brow lowered.

"Yes, but Jayden's our guest, and it's his birthday."

"It's fine. I don't mind." Jayden forced a smile that looked warmer than it felt as he slipped Simon's half onto his plate.

"That's very kind of you."

He shrugged. He had no choice. He wolfed down the half slice, wiped his face with a napkin, and then passed his plate to Mrs. Morgan. "Thank you."

"You've got a good appetite, son." Mr. Morgan ruffled his hair.

"You would too if you ate frozen meals every night," Angie said.

"Guess I would." Mr. Morgan smiled at her. "So where are you three planning on riding?"

Angie shrugged. "Not sure yet. Maybe across the stream and then up to Gooseneck Gorge."

Mr. Morgan shifted his gaze to Jayden. "Have you ridden before, son?"

Jayden straightened. "A little."

"Take it easy, then." Mr. Morgan turned his attention to Angie and lowered his voice. "Let Jayden ride Misty—she'll be the best horse for him."

"Will do." Angie pushed her chair back and looked at Jayden. "I'll help Mom with the dishes and then we'll go. Oh, and I need to give you your present." Her face expanded into a broad grin.

"It's okay. I'll help Mom. You three go." Mr. Morgan turned

to Jessica, who hadn't said a word right through lunch and had barely eaten a bite, and placed his hands on her shoulders. "Sure you won't go, sweetie?"

She shook her head. Her face was so pale and thin.

Mr. Morgan let out a sigh before turning back to Angie. "Be back in time for dinner, and ride carefully."

Angie threw her arms around him. "We will. Thank you."

"Enjoy your ride, son." He nodded at Jayden before turning to Simon, his expression growing serious. "And no shenanigans."

"Yes, Dad." Simon hung his head and looked down at his feet.

"Come on, Jayden. Let's get ready." Grabbing his hand, Angie dragged him inside. "Mom said you can have the down-stairs room. Got your clothes?"

He nodded. "Yep."

"I won't be long." She squeezed his hand and disappeared upstairs.

Jayden stepped into the spare room which Blake, Jessica's boyfriend, had been using before he went off to College. The room was almost as big as his entire apartment. A queen-size bed dominated the room, which also contained an old oak dresser, a dark-brown leather wing chair made brighter by the addition of several neatly arranged lime-green cushions and a throw rug, and a whole wall of family portraits.

He quickly changed out of his work clothes and slipped on a pair of thick, blue denim jeans and the long sleeved checked shirt he'd bought especially for the afternoon's ride. The shirt still had the fold lines on it, and felt itchy as his arms slid into it. He grimaced. He should have washed it. Lastly, he put on the leather boots he'd been saving up for for weeks. Ariat boots. Comfortable and trendy. All he needed now was a cowboy hat. He glanced at himself in the full-length mirror. *Not bad.* Leaning closer, he ran his hand down his cheek and inspected the two-day-old growth on his face. A sudden thought flashed through his mind. Dad would hardly recognize him now. He hadn't even begun shaving before he'd left with Mom. He swallowed the lump that had suddenly lodged in his throat. He'd have to write another letter.

"Jayden, are you ready?" Angie's voice sounded outside the room.

"Yep. Coming." He quickly grabbed his bag and opened the door.

Dressed in a white, snug fitting shirt with the sleeves rolled up to her elbows, Angie stood holding a box wrapped in purple paper with a big bow on top. She held it out, a beaming smile lighting her face. "Happy birthday, Jayden."

"Thank you!" He took the box from her and carried it to the sofa in the living area just outside his room.

"Can you guess what it is?" Her eyes glistened, and she held her hands together tightly as she jigged on the spot.

Jayden shook the parcel gently. No rattle. Fairly light. He had no idea. He lifted his eyes. "Give me a clue."

"No. Just open it." She looked at him with expectant eyes.

What if he didn't like whatever it was? He'd have to pretend. He couldn't let her down, she was so excited about it. He began by carefully undoing the bow, and then ran his finger under the tape on one side and then the other. Finally the paper came off, almost intact, revealing a brown box that looked very much like it might hold a hat. He lifted his gaze, a slow grin forming on his face. "Is this what I think it is?"

"What do you think it is?" she asked playfully.

"A cowboy hat?"

She nodded eagerly. "Yes. Open it!"

He lifted the lid and pulled out a black Bullhide Leather cowboy hat. He took his time to inspect it before he placed it on his head. "How's it look?"

"Cute!" Angie giggled. "Come and take a look." Dragging him back into the room, she stood him in front of the mirror, and stretching on her tippy-toes, peeked over his shoulder.

He caught her eye. The light from the window bounced off her copper red hair making it shine, and her eyes danced with excitement. His pulse quickened. Maybe now was the time to tell her. Turning around slowly, he placed his hands on her hips, his heart thumping so loudly she had to hear it.

"Do you like it?" She looked at him eagerly.

"I love it." He gulped. "Just like I…

"Ange, are you coming?" Simon appeared in the doorway but stopped with a jerk. "Whoops. Sorry." He took a step back.

Jayden let out a frustrated sigh. *Trust Simon to get in the way.*

She held his gaze for another second before turning her head towards her brother. "Yes, Simon, we're coming."

Jayden took her hand and squeezed it. It was all he could do in front of her brother.

"Glad you like it." Angie smiled sweetly at him. "Come on, let's go."

. . .

SHORTLY AFTER, the three were saddled up and were headed towards the mountains. Angie took the lead on a brown gelding called Rusty, Jayden was in the middle on Misty, a pie-bald mare with a gentle nature, and Simon brought up the rear on a dark mare called Midnight. The trail narrowed quickly, and before long the ranch was out of sight, and they weaved their way slowly higher towards the foothills of the mountain range that sat behind the Morgan's ranch.

Misty was sure-footed, and Jayden felt comfortable in his new attire, including his cowboy hat and boots. Angie was an expert horse rider, but had promised to take it easy since he hadn't ridden in a while. In fact, he hadn't really ridden a horse at all; just a pony at the local Show, but he wasn't going to tell her that. How difficult could it be?

They trotted along in silence, with just the occasional word spoken between them until the narrow trail opened up to a meadow full of green grass and colorful wildflowers. Angie stopped and Jayden pulled Misty up alongside her. He gazed in awe at the wide open expanse. In the distance, the mountains stood rocky and stark against the deep-blue Montana sky. His thoughts turned to this week's Bible study, where they'd discussed the complexity of God's creation and the amazing detail in even the very smallest of animals. The more he learned, the more he was convinced that all of this just couldn't have happened by accident.

"Beautiful, isn't it?" Angie turned her head and caught his eye.

"Sure is."

Simon leaned forward, raising his reins as he looked around Jayden and challenged Angie. "Race?"

Angie glared at him. "Remember what Dad said? No shenanigans."

Simon rolled his eyes. "Well, I'm off—see you down there." He kicked the sides of his horse with his boots; Midnight reared and took off. Simon moved effortlessly in time with the galloping horse.

Jayden gazed longingly after him. It'd be such fun, riding fast, the wind whipping through his hair, the sound of the horse thudding across the hard ground. His heart beat faster. "Come on, Ange, let's go."

Her eyes popped. "You can't be serious. You'll fall off."

"No, I won't. Coming?" He lifted the reins and gave Misty a gentle kick. She took off, throwing him backwards before he managed to pull himself upright. He steadied his feet in the stirrups, stiffening his legs to stand, just like he'd seen in the movies, and held on. His heart thumped. She wasn't going as fast as Midnight, but it was fast enough. The thud of her hooves sent thrills through his body. This was even better than jet-skiing or snow-boarding.

Angie's horse caught him and galloped alongside. Jayden turned his head and gave Angie a beaming smile. She didn't return it. Her lips had flat-lined, and her glare was so intense he thought her eyes would pop out.

Girls. Why couldn't he have some fun? It'd been too long. *Way too long.* Jayden turned his head to the front and focused on staying upright. Angie could like it or lump it. He wasn't going to fall off. Adrenaline coursed through his veins like a bolt of lightning that kept coming. He geed Misty up, urging her to go faster. She responded. The exhilaration was like nothing he'd ever experienced.

Simon was up ahead and had brought Midnight to a slow canter.

The ground had become rockier as the foothills of the mountains loomed ahead. Now all Jayden had to do was slow Misty down without falling off. It was taking all his effort to hold on; how was he going to pull the reins in? He tried, but almost lost his balance. His pulse raced. *She's not going to stop... there's water up ahead.* His heart beat faster. *Surely she'll stop... don't horses do that?* He clenched his jaw. All of a sudden his legs felt like jelly. The stream loomed. Misty wasn't slowing. His breaths came faster. He braced himself. *This is going to hurt.* He swallowed hard. One last time he tried to pull the reins in. As he did, Angie reached out and grabbed them, somehow slowing both horses at the same time.

"Stupid, Jayden. Stupid. You could have killed yourself." Her chest heaved. Her face had turned almost as red as her hair.

Hanging his head, Jayden panted as he tried to catch his breath. *Yes, what was I thinking?* He raised his head. "Sorry Ange, I shouldn't have done that."

"No, you shouldn't."

"But it was fun." He shot her a cheeky grin.

She shook her head, but then burst out laughing. "Don't ever let Dad know you did that."

"I won't."

"That was a close call," Simon said as he pulled Midnight to a halt beside them, a smug look on his face. "Don't know how to stop, Jayden?"

Jayden drew a breath. *Count to ten.* "No, but you can show me if you want."

Simon shrugged. "Maybe later."

"Okay, now we're all here, *safely*, let's have a drink and then we'll cross and climb up to the ridge." Angie reached into her saddle bag and drew out her water canteen.

Jayden followed suit, gulping greedily as the cool water slid down his throat. He hadn't realized how thirsty he was.

"Keep some for later." Her voice had softened.

"Okay, but can't we fill up?"

She raised an eyebrow. "Here? No, you never know what's pooped in the water."

"Bears?"

She laughed. "No bears around here, but there's elk and the odd moose, and loads of beavers."

"Will we see any?"

"Maybe, we'll keep an eye out."

"Okay." He smiled at her. They'd survived their first tiff and she'd forgiven him for acting like a goose. He'd have to act more grown up around her. He really had been stupid.

The track to the ridge was windy and narrow. Simon led the way, followed by Jayden, with Angie bringing up the rear. Half an hour after crossing the stream, they reached the top and dismounted.

Jayden stood and gazed around. *Magic. Absolutely magic.* In the distance, snow-capped mountains stretched as far as the eye could see, reminding him of the Remarkables in New Zealand, and sending a pang of guilt through his body. He should never have disappeared like he had. What had he been thinking? He pushed the memory away. He was here now, gazing at the Rocky Mountains with the girl he loved holding his hand. What could be better than that? He pulled Angie close and wrapped his arms around her in a bear hug. As he brushed a strand of loose hair off her face, his pulse quickened. They shouldn't be doing this. They'd agreed, but she was so beautiful, and the mountains were so breathtaking, and the ride had been exhilarating. He just wanted to kiss her. He gazed into her eyes and began lowering his face.

"Come on you two, stop being so lovey-dovey." Simon stood to Jayden's left, his nose wrinkling and his lip curling.

Jayden dropped his arms and bit his lip. He could get angry with Simon if he wasn't careful. Why did he have to come? Jayden sucked in a breath and glared at him.

Angie squeezed Jayden's hand and leaned her head against his shoulder. "It's okay. Probably better he's here." She angled her head and spoke quietly.

She was probably right. They could easily get carried away. *But still...*

"Let's have a snack before we head back." She let go of his hand and opened her saddle bag, pulling out a plastic lunch box before choosing a flat rock to sit on.

Jayden sat beside her; Simon chose a different rock a few feet away.

"These look great." Jayden's mouth watered at the pile of homemade cookies sitting in the box.

"Mom made them this morning."

"You're very lucky." A sudden wave of sadness washed over him. It must be so good to have a mother like Mrs. Morgan. Mom had never been like her. She hated cooking. And Tessa, well, she tried, but it wasn't the same. Jayden swallowed the lump in his throat. Dad had told him about the new baby they were expecting. He hoped Tessa didn't lose it this time.

He took a chocolate chip cookie and nibbled on it as he

gazed at the mountains. In the distance, an eagle soared on a current. *Magic. It must be so cool up there.*

"Do you think you'll ever go back?" Turning her head, Angie looked at him as she drew her knees up and wrapped her arms around them.

Jayden held her gaze for a second and then looked down. That was a good question. One he'd been thinking about a lot. But no, he couldn't go back. He was getting fed up with Mom, and in fact, after this morning, he was almost ready to forget about her, but how could he leave Angie? He raised his head. "No, I don't think so, not for a long time."

"Your mom?" Angie raised an eyebrow.

He nodded slowly. How could he tell Angie it was her, not his mom, keeping him here?

"You know, she doesn't deserve you, the way she's treated you."

He shrugged. "But she's my mom."

"But you've also got a dad and a step-mom who really miss you."

He inhaled slowly. She was right. But how could he go home and leave her behind?

A small smile grew on her face. "Plus you'll have a baby brother or sister soon. I'm sure they'll want you there for that."

His shoulders slumped. "Sounds like you want to get rid of me."

Angie's forehead puckered, her expression growing serious. She reached out and placed her hand lightly on his leg. "I don't want to get rid of you, but I've been thinking that maybe you should go home before the baby comes."

"But what about us?" A heavy weight settled on his heart.

Angie's eyes misted over. She brushed them quickly with the back of her hand. "When we started going out, I didn't know much about your family, but now I do, I think you should be with them." She paused, sucking in another breath and swallowing hard. "You shouldn't be here with me, or even your mom." She wriggled closer to him and placed her arm around his shoulder. "I'm sure my mom and dad would look out for her."

Jayden kicked some dirt with his boot. He couldn't leave Angie. *He loved her.* His heart beat faster. No, he couldn't leave.

"Angie, I don't want to leave you." His voice caught in his throat as tears pricked his eyes. Surely they weren't breaking up?

"We're only young, Jayden. We shouldn't be planning our whole lives around each other."

Tears rolled down his cheek as he held her gaze. "Are you breaking up with me?"

She exhaled slowly. "No. I'm just saying you need to make the right decision, and that maybe you shouldn't even be thinking about me."

"But Ange," he gazed into her eyes," I..." he gulped. He couldn't say it.

"Let's leave it for now." She blinked back the tears wedged in her eyes. "There's plenty of time to think about it—the baby's not due until Christmas." Her eyes lit up and she attempted a smile. "Maybe you could surprise them and go home for Christmas?"

Jayden brightened. He pulled her close and kissed the side of her head. "Maybe you could come with me?"

CHAPTER 7 | 63

Her mouth fell open. "I… I don't know what Mom and Dad would think about that."

He inhaled slowly as he stroked her hair. "Think about it?"

A moment of silence passed between them. She held his gaze.

His pulse quickened. If she came home with him, that would be the answer to everything.

"I'll think about it." She gave him one of her dazzling smiles.

Jayden sighed. He'd have to be happy with that for now.

THE RIDE back was much more subdued than the ride out. Jayden was lost in thought almost the whole way. What would it be like to take Angie home to Australia to meet Dad and Tessa? And to meet his new little brother or sister? But would she leave her own mom and dad, and Jessica, and Jess's new baby, and come with him? He glanced at her as they approached the ranch. *What would he do if she didn't?*

CHAPTER 8

$\mathcal{M}$r. Morgan was outside in the yard hanging fairy lights between the trees when the three arrived back after putting the horses away. Several tables had been laid out to one side, and a large fire was set in a hollow away from the house.

Jayden looked at Angie, his eyebrows drawn. "So... what's happening?"

She crossed her legs at the ankle and held her hands together in front of her, gazing at the ground before raising her head slowly. "Nothing, really. We're just having a few people over."

He narrowed his eyes further. "Thought it was just us for dinner."

She lifted her chin and gave him a playful smile. "I never said that."

No, she hadn't. He'd just assumed.

"So, who's coming?"

"Don't worry. Just a few of the youth, and Uncle John and Aunt Mary from next door, and our cousins, that's all."

"It's not for my birthday, is it?"

She sidled up to him. "And if it was?" She held both his hands and looked coyly at him.

Jayden inhaled slowly. He'd rather not spend his birthday with people he didn't know well, but what could he do? "Guess it'd be okay, but I'd rather spend it with you."

Angie slapped his wrist lightly. "Jayden."

"It's true."

"Well, they're all nice people, and we'll have fun, you'll see."

"Mmm." He still wasn't quite sure how to feel about having a party sprung on him.

"How was your ride?" Mr. Morgan stepped off the ladder, folded it up, and then placed it on his shoulder as he headed towards them.

Jayden glanced at Angie. She wouldn't say anything, but would Simon?

"It was great, Dad. No problems at all." She sounded a little too innocent, as if she were trying too hard to convince him.

"And how did you go, Jayden?"

"Good, thanks. My butt's a bit sore, that's all." Jayden felt his bottom before testing his legs. "And my legs are a bit wobbly, but it was worth it. Didn't see any moose, though."

Mr. Morgan chuckled. "I'll take you out one day and we'll find some. Would you like that?"

"Yes, sir, that'd be great."

"We could have a boy's camp-out. Do some fishing, spot some bears. I'll plan it."

"Sounds good." *But not if Simon's coming...*

Mr. Morgan continued on his way.

Angie glanced at her watch. "We'd better get cleaned up. They'll be here soon."

Jayden's shoulders slumped as he nodded. So much for spending time alone with her.

JAYDEN TOOK a shower downstairs and then pulled on some clean jeans and a white T-shirt. Thinking Angie would probably be a while, he walked over to the wall lined with family photos and cast his eye over them. They were a very close family, but then, he already knew that. Angie and Jess could almost be twins. Both had copper-red curly hair, but Angie's eyes were green, while Jess's were hazel. Jayden sighed. How could he expect Angie to leave when her sister was having a baby, even if it was only for a visit? Maybe she'd come after Jess had the baby. Or maybe she wouldn't come at all. If that was the case, he'd stay. She said they were only young, but he loved her. His life had changed in such a short time, and he couldn't imagine life without her. As he gazed into her smiling eyes, his heart beat with love for her. He'd have to choose between Angie and Dad—he couldn't have them both.

A soft knock on the door interrupted Jayden's thoughts. He quickly stepped back from the photos.

"Come in."

The door opened. Angie stood in the doorway, smelling amazing. She was wearing the perfume he'd given her, and she'd pulled her hair up into a top knot. A few strands spiraled down the sides of her cheeks. He wanted to touch them. She was wearing make-up, and her eyes sparkled even more than normal. Maybe she didn't know what effect she had on him, but all he wanted to do was hold her tight and kiss her.

He inhaled slowly. No way could he kiss Angela Morgan the way he wanted to, especially in her parents' house. He'd have to control himself. He stepped towards her and took her hand. "Ange, you look beautiful."

She gave him a coy smile. "Thanks. You're not bad yourself."

He took another deep breath. "I was just looking at these photos." He placed his arm lightly on her shoulder and turned her to face the wall.

She pointed out a photo of when she was a toddler and laughed. She and Jess were wearing the same outfits. "Mom used to do that all the time."

Standing beside her, hearing her laugh and breathing in her perfume, Jayden grew dizzy. Maybe he could steal a kiss? His pulse quickened as they studied the most recent photo. Blake had his arm around Jess. If Blake could be in a Morgan family photo, why couldn't he?

Jayden turned her slowly towards him. He held a finger to her chin and tilted her face. His stomach tightened. Her eyes met his and held. His heart pounded. He gulped and cleared his throat. "Can I..." Jayden gulped. "Can I kiss you, Angie?"

She blinked and swallowed. "Jayden..." Her chest heaved. "You know we can't."

His heart fell.

She lifted her hand to his cheek. "I'm sorry, but we can't."

He placed his hand on hers. "But I love you, Angie." The words slipped out of his mouth.

Her eyes widened, her body stiffening. Seconds passed.

Why did he say that? She dropped her hand, but her gaze remained steady. "Jayden…"

He stepped closer, placing his hands on her shoulders. "I'm sorry. I shouldn't have said that."

Her lip trembled. She swallowed again, her eyes still fixed on his. "We're too young to feel like that."

Tears stung his eyes. No they weren't. He loved her. They weren't too young to know true love.

She stepped closer and hugged him, resting her head against his chest before lifting her face. "Let's not spoil what we've got?"

Jayden drew in a long, slow breath before nodding. He swallowed hard and released his breath. "I'm sorry. I won't say it again."

She smiled at him before kissing her finger and placing it on his lips.

He breathed a sigh of relief. At least he hadn't lost her.

AT THE SOUND of cars pulling up outside, Angie took Jayden's hand and led him outside to greet their friends. A group of eight young people from the church had arrived in two cars. Gareth and Rachel, Matt, Dave and Rosy were amongst them.

Gareth extended his hand. "Happy birthday, Jayden."

Jayden took Gareth's hand and shook it. "Thanks."

The others followed suit.

"What's for dinner, Ange?" Dave sniffed the air. "Smells good, whatever it is."

"Ribs, what else would you expect from my dad?" Angie let out a small laugh.

Dave nodded. "Your dad's ribs are the best."

"They're about the one thing he knows how to cook." She glanced towards her father who stood in front of the large outdoor barbecue turning ribs while chatting with Pastor Graham. Jayden had to agree with Dave—his mouth watered at the aroma of smoking ribs wafting in the air towards them.

"Time for a game of pool before dinner?" Gareth asked.

"Sure," Angie replied. "You know where it is."

"Like a game?" Gareth asked Jayden.

Not really, but what could he do? "Okay, that'd be great."

Jayden squeezed Angie's hand before stepping away from her and heading towards the pool room with the boys. Why couldn't they have done something together? Besides, the boys would all be better than him.

Dave headed straight for the CD player and put music on that Jayden hadn't heard before.

Gareth pulled two cues off the wall and handed one to Jayden, raising his brow. "You and me against Dave and Matt?"

Jayden shrugged. "Guess so. I'm not good at it, though."

"Doesn't matter. It's just for fun."

"Okay, but don't say I didn't warn you." Jayden took the chalk Gareth handed him and chalked the end of his cue. At least he knew that much.

Gareth arranged the balls in the rack and then stood aside and picked up his cue. "Who wants to break?" His gaze shifted between the three other boys.

"Jayden, since it's his birthday," Matt said.

Jayden shook his head. "No, you go."

Matt shrugged. "Okay. As long as you're sure."

"Yeah. Go for it."

Matt stepped to the edge of the table and placed the white ball in front of the others. He lined up his cue and then paused for a second before releasing it with a quick flick of his wrist. The white ball smashed into the others, sending them flying across the table and into the walls before they bounced back and settled. The only ball he pocketed was the red striped ball. He then lined up what looked like an easy shot, but missed. He straightened and then shrugged. "Your turn, Jayden."

Jayden drew a slow breath. His hands shook as he lined up his cue. He was about to take the shot when he changed his mind at the last second. He'd get a better angle by aiming for the green ball. He moved around the table to his left, lined his cue up with the white ball and the green, slid the cue slowly back between his fingers, and then released it with a snap. The white ball hit the green one cleanly, sending it straight into the end pocket. Jayden released his breath.

"Thought you said you couldn't play?" Gareth slapped him on the back.

Jayden shrugged and tried to hide the grin growing on his face. "Beginner's luck." But when he pocketed another ball, the others said it couldn't have been.

He relaxed and watched the others, joking and laughing with them, and for a short while, forgot about Angie. He and Gareth went on to win the game, and Jayden was just about to take what could be the winning shot in the second game when Angie and Rachel appeared at the door. His mouth went dry. What if he missed? His heart pounded. All eyes were on him. He glanced up and met Angie's gaze. Leaning on the door-frame with folded arms, her eye held an expectant sparkle. But he couldn't let her distract him. He inhaled slowly and returned his attention to the table. He'd been playing well, much better than he thought he would, but this was a tricky shot. He had to get the eight-ball to ricochet off the wall at exactly the right angle to pocket it. If he got it wrong, Dave would get a shot at it.

The only sound came from the CD player as he steadied his cue, lining it up carefully. He made a practice shot, and then adjusted the angle slightly. It was only a game, but with Angie watching, he really needed to pocket this ball.

He held his breath and eased the cue back. The cue snapped forward, hitting the white ball cleanly. It clipped the eight-ball on the left side just where he'd intended, sending it off to the right. The eight-ball hit the cushion, ricocheted, but lost momentum as it arced around and headed towards the far pocket. It didn't have enough legs. He should have hit it harder. No one moved. The ball slowed, stopping just in front of the pocket. His shoulders slumped. A half inch more, that's all it needed. Dave would easily pocket it now.

"Great shot, Jayden." Angie stepped into the room and stood beside him, placing her arm lightly on his back.

Straightening, Jayden winced. "It could have been better."

He slipped his arm around her waist as Dave lined up his cue to down the eight-ball. As expected, Dave snapped the cue onto the white ball, and within a split second, the game was over.

Dave and Matt high-fived, and then they both extended their hands to Jayden and Gareth. "Great game, guys. Thanks." Dave winked at Angie. "You didn't put him off or anything."

Maybe Angie watching had put him off, but he wasn't going to let her think that. He pulled her closer. "No, she didn't."

"Thanks Jayden, that's sweet of you." Angie popped a kiss onto his cheek, and all was forgotten. "Anyway, the ribs are ready."

"Cool," Dave said as he placed his cue on the rack on the wall. "I could eat a whole bull."

"I think Dad cooked enough for you to do that." Angie laughed. "Let's go."

THE SPREAD WAS AMAZING; so much food Jayden wouldn't need to eat for a week. He piled his plate high with the best ribs he'd ever smelled, and a teeny amount of salad, only because Angie made him. He would have been happy to have just eaten ribs like Dave was doing. Having a girlfriend had its drawbacks.

He and Angie sat on a bench seat under a huge fir tree and perched their plates on their laps. The others formed a semicircle on either side of them and did the same. The adults were all eating together at a table, and Simon sat on the ground with his cousins.

A hush fell over the group as Jessica joined them and sat on the bench beside Angie. Her plate only held a couple of ribs and a small amount of salad and potato. Angie placed her arm around Jess's shoulder and gave her a squeeze. Seemed like no one really knew what to say.

Rachel slid to the edge of her seat and began talking with Jessica and Angie. Everyone else resumed their conversations. Jayden sat and listened, taken aback at the topic of conversation—last week's Bible study. So different to the party he'd gone to with Roger, where the kids had just wanted to get high and make out. This group knew how to have fun, but they also seemed to know who they were and what they believed in, and they were more than happy to talk about it. *Amazing.*

He listened with interest. He'd been reading ahead in the study guide, and had checked out as much non-Biblical material as he could find on the Internet that confirmed the historical happenings recorded in the Bible. The amount of proof for events he'd always assumed were just made-up stories astounded him.

When the boys began talking about the origin of the universe, his ears pricked up. He'd been trying to get his head around what he'd been reading... that there were only two possibilities for anything that exists. Either it's always been, and is therefore uncaused, or that it has a beginning, caused by something else. Things couldn't be self-caused, because they'd already have to exist in order to cause something else. *The law of causality.* He'd never thought about that before starting the study, but it was true. Nothing had ever come into being without someone or something making it. Not a pen, not an animal, not a plant. And not even the universe, so it seemed.

Scientists agreed the universe was expanding, and therefore it had to have a beginning, but they disagreed on how it came about. But how could *no one* create something out of nothing? It made more sense that *someone* had. A thought suddenly struck him. If God was real, as he was beginning to think He was, who had made God? Or had He always been? More study was needed.

"I was blown away by the way the whole universe is held in place," Gareth said. He leaned back and gazed upwards. "All that matter up there, just hanging together. If just one thing got out of place, like what happened with Apollo 13, we'd all be gone."

"Yeah, and what about that info about the amoeba? The tiniest thing, but it has more information in its DNA than all thirty volumes of the Encyclopedia Britannica." Dave shook his head. "How did that happen if it wasn't God?"

"Yeah, I don't understand why people don't believe," Gareth said, putting his plate on the ground.

"Makes no sense to me." Dave shrugged as he picked up another rib and tore into it with his teeth.

"What about you, Jayden? How are you finding the study?" Gareth shifted in his seat and faced him.

Jayden stiffened. It was one thing to read and study in private, another to talk about it openly. He swallowed and leaned back. He had to say something. He let out a breath. *Here goes...* "It's...it's really interesting, but I need to read more."

"Yeah, there's so much info, it kind of blows your mind," Gareth said. "But you know, a lot of people read too much and even though they end up believing God's real, they don't go any further. And that's really sad."

Jayden wriggled on his chair. Gareth might be right, but he wasn't ready to do anything yet, and he wasn't going to let them pressure him.

"Hey." Angie turned and placed her arm around his shoulder. "Enjoy your ribs?"

"Yeah, they were great." He smiled at her, glad she'd interrupted the conversation, even though he'd enjoyed listening.

"Mom's got some dessert later, but I think it's time to light the fire. Come and help?"

Jayden nodded. Maybe he'd get some time alone with her after all.

CHAPTER 9

Seated around the fire a short while later, Jayden placed his arm around Angie's shoulder and pulled her close. Gareth had brought his guitar and was strumming away, not playing anything in particular, but his finger-work was amazing. Jayden almost wished he'd brought his, but then he wouldn't be able to hold Angie.

She looked up and smiled. "Enjoying your birthday?"

Nodding, he returned her smile and kissed her forehead. Yes, he was. It'd been the best birthday he'd ever had. The only sour note had been Mom not remembering. It saddened him every time he thought about her. She'd changed so much since the day she whisked him away in Luke Emerson's private jet. Now she could hardly look after herself. She'd turned into a sad, pitiful woman. It was a wonder Buck was still happy to have her around.

Angie leaned back and gazed heavenward. "The stars are awesome, aren't they?"

Jayden tilted his head and looked up. They sure were.

She rested her head on his shoulder. "You know they reckon there's about a hundred billion stars in our galaxy, and just to get to the nearest star it'd take over two hundred thousand years to get there? I can't even begin to imagine how long that is."

He shook his head. "Yeah, it's pretty amazing stuff."

Angie continued gazing at the sky, seemingly lost in its wonder. Her voice was dreamy. "The heavens declare the glory of God; the skies proclaim the work of His hands." Even though she spoke softly, the awe in her voice was obvious.

Jayden's eyebrows lifted. "You know that by heart?"

She nodded. "Yep. Sunday School classes."

As he continued staring at the night sky, questions triggered by the earlier conversation floated through his mind. Eventually he turned and looked at Angie. "Can I ask you a question?"

She turned her head. "Sure."

"Who made God?"

Her brows furrowed and then she chuckled. "No one, silly. He's always been. He's God." The look on her face made him laugh. Her faith was so simple.

"Mmm… that's what I was starting to think."

"You can have a chat with Dad or Pastor Graham if you want. They know more than me."

Jayden shrugged. "Maybe later."

"Okay." She settled back in his arms before sitting with a start. "Jayden, you do know God loves you, don't you? He's not just up there, He can be in here, too." She placed her hand on her chest, her brows wrinkling as she held his gaze.

*Here goes...*he drew in a breath. She was going to pressure him. "I'm not sure how all that works."

"Do you want to know?" She angled her head.

He shrugged again. He kind of did, but he wasn't ready. "I guess so. But not now."

"Okay." She smiled at him and then rested her head back against his chest.

He looked back at the sky. The stars appeared brighter, as if they were shining down on him. His heart quickened. *Maybe God was sending him a message.*

AFTER EVERYONE LEFT, Jayden and Angie helped her parents clean up, and once the kitchen was tidy again, they sat around the kitchen table with mugs of hot chocolate. Jessica had gone to bed, but Simon was still up.

"Did you have a good day, Jayden?" Mrs. Morgan pulled out a chair and joined them.

"Yes, I did. Thank you." He gave her a warm smile. She really was the best mom anyone could have.

"Our pleasure. We thought you might like having some young folk around for your birthday." Her face grew serious. "You must be missing your friends and family back home."

Jayden let out a sigh. The only real friend he had back home was Neil, but they'd lost touch of late. Neil had taken up with another group at school, and besides, they had nothing in common anymore. Neil was still a school kid, and had no idea about working to support himself. *But Dad and Tessa?* Yes, if he were honest, he was missing them more as each day passed, and he still got a lump in his throat whenever he thought about how he'd treated them.

He stared at the froth sitting on top of his hot chocolate and toyed with his mug before looking up and meeting Mrs. Morgan's soft eyes. "Yeah, a bit." His voice choked. Maybe it was the whole emotional bit with Mom, and then the horse ride, and then telling Angie he loved her, followed by the discussion about God, but whatever it was, all of a sudden his cheeks grew warm. A lump formed in his throat as burning pain clutched his heart. Within moments, tears stung his eyes and then rolled down his cheeks.

Angie leaned closer and squeezed his hand. Mrs. Morgan jumped up and wrapped her arms around him.

"It's okay, son. It's perfectly understandable." Mr. Morgan slid a box of tissues across the table.

Jayden sniffed and tried to stop his tears. His chest heaved as he sucked in some quick breaths.

Simon stared at him across the table, his eyes wide, as if he didn't believe that a seventeen-year-old boy would let himself cry in front of his girlfriend's parents.

"I'm sorry…" Jayden sniffed again and swallowed hard, "it just all got to me." He squeezed his eyes tight and tried desperately to control himself. How could this have happened? And in front of Simon, of all people.

Mrs. Morgan gave him another squeeze. "You can talk about it if you want, Jayden, but it's okay if you don't."

Jayden nodded. "Thanks." His voice was croaky and broken. "Give me a minute."

"No problem, there's no hurry." Mrs. Morgan smiled at him and then took her seat again.

"Thank you." He gave her the best smile he could manage.

The tick from the clock on the far wall seemed louder all of a sudden. Ten o'clock. It'd be Sunday afternoon back home. Jayden's pulse quickened. *Maybe I should call Dad?* It had been almost a year since he'd left, and he hadn't spoken to Dad or Tessa in all that time. His stomach tightened. Could he do it? He let out a slow sigh, his shoulders sagging. *No...*

"Would you like us to pray for you, son?" Mr. Morgan leaned forward, his folded arms resting on the table. His eyes were warm, just like Angie's.

Jayden took a deep breath but his heart beat faster. Surprisingly, he did. Nodding, he pushed back a fresh round of tears.

Mr. and Mrs. Morgan both stood and walked around the table, placing their hands lightly on his shoulders. Angie reached for his hand and turned to face him. Simon remained seated, shifting uneasily in his chair.

Something unfamiliar fluttered inside Jayden's heart.

"Let's pray." Mr. Morgan's voice was warm and reassuring. "Lord God, we bring Jayden to You tonight. Such a special young man who's been through so much. He's hurting, Lord, but we know You can give him new life and new hope, and that You can heal all the hurts and disappointments in his life. Lord, we pray he'll open his heart to You, and welcome You in. Reveal Yourself to him, dear Lord, that he might see You and know that You're not only real, but that You love him more than anything."

Mrs. Morgan took over. "And we also pray, dear Lord, for reconciliation between Jayden and his family, especially with his dad and step-mom. I can't even imagine how they must be feeling, so I pray You'll comfort them and give them hope that one day soon they'll be reunited." Her voice choked, and she paused for a moment. She swallowed hard. The only sound, apart from Jayden's beating heart, was the ticking of the clock. "And dear Lord, we also pray for Jayden's mother. Lord, no-one's beyond your help, so we pray for her, that she might start looking beyond herself and reach out to You, and that one day she might also come to know You as her Personal Lord and Savior. Knock on the door of her heart, Lord, just as You've been knocking on Jayden's. Thank You, dear Lord, in Jesus' precious name, Amen."

Jayden tried to control his emotions. His heart felt constricted, as if something had clutched it and weighed it down. He could barely breathe. Angie squeezed his hand again. Mr. and Mrs. Morgan stood behind him with their hands still on his shoulders. He thought he'd feel better after being prayed for, but he felt worse, as if something inside him was fighting.

"Are you okay?" Angie leaned closer, her head touching his.

Jayden lifted his head slowly and turned his face. "I...I think so. I just need to go to bed."

"Good idea, son." Mr. Morgan patted his back gently.

Jayden forced a smile and nodded as he stood slowly.

"Sleep well, Jayden." Mrs. Morgan wrapped her arms around him again, pulling him tight.

All he could manage was a small smile. He just wanted to bury his head in his pillow and cry.

Angie walked with him to his room. When they reached the door, she looked up and gazed into his eyes. "Jayden, remember that God's not just up there," she raised her eyes to the ceiling, "but He can be in here, too." She placed her hand on her chest. "He loves you."

He nodded slowly. For a long moment he held her gaze. He didn't trust himself to speak. He just needed to be on his own.

Angie stretched up and placed a kiss on his cheek, and for once, he was happy with that. "Good night, Jayden. See you in the morning."

He pulled her close, holding her tight for a short moment before releasing her. He gulped and cleared his throat. "Thanks Angie." His voice croaked. "It's been a great day." He squeezed back fresh tears as she smiled at him and turned to walk away.

JAYDEN ENTERED his room and closed the door. Sitting on his bed, he held his head in his hands. If only the noise would stop. His chest heaved. He had to know if what Angie had said was true. Could God really live in his heart?

He tried to settle his thoughts. All along he'd determined not to get caught up with emotion, and it annoyed him that he'd let his guard down. Right now his heart felt raw, vulnerable. How could he know for sure if it was just emotion he was feeling, or if God really was trying to get through to him?

After several more moments, he raised his head and inhaled slowly. Sitting on the shelf beside his bed, an old, well-used Bible caught his attention. He reached for it and flipped it open. So many pages; so many words. He needed more than the verses he'd been reading about God. He needed to discover how to know God.

A few scrap pieces of paper, like bookmarks, poked out of the Bible. He flicked to the first one and read the verse in Isaiah Chapter 55 that someone had highlighted. *'Seek the Lord while He may be found; call on Him while he is near.'*

His heart quickened. *But how do you find Him?* He flicked to the next bookmarked page and found another verse highlighted; Jeremiah chapter 29, verses 11 to 14: *"'For I know the plans I have for you,' declares the Lord, 'plans to prosper you and not to harm you, plans to give you hope and a future. Then you will call on me and come and pray to me, and I will listen to you. You will seek me and find me when you seek me with all your heart. I will be found by you,' declares the Lord, 'and will bring you back from captivity.'"*

The answer was clear. He had to seek God with all his heart. He closed the Bible and knelt beside his bed, something he hadn't done for many years. He drew a long, slow breath and closed his eyes. A longing deep within him welled up and spilled out in the form of tears. He really didn't need to say anything, but eventually he managed a few words. His voice was little more than a whisper. *"God, please show me how I can know You. Please show me the way."*

CHAPTER 10

*W*ith so much on his mind and his heart, Jayden hadn't expected to sleep the night of his birthday, so when the first rays of sunlight stole through the window the following morning, he blinked. Sunday morning, and he didn't need to go to work. And he was at Angie's place. *Even better.* But then the events of the night before flashed through his mind. Had he really broken down in front of her entire family? A heaviness grew in his chest. How could he face them this morning? Especially Simon. He needed to see Angie.

Although tempted to stay in bed and hide, he eventually climbed out and dressed in jeans and a T-shirt. He walked quietly towards the kitchen, his shoulders falling as he peeked in. Mrs. Morgan and Jessica were seated at the table, their heads close together, talking quietly.

He backed up slowly. Maybe they hadn't seen him. He turned and inched along the hallway to a side door, which he opened very quietly, and snuck outside. He shivered as the door clicked behind him. The sun hadn't yet warmed the air, but its rays, filtering through the trees in the distance, promised another lovely day ahead. Maybe a walk would do him good. Get his mind sorted. But as he stood, drawing in the crisp country air, the sound of cows mooing gently reached his ears from the barn to the left of the ranch.

Jayden wandered over to the barn and peeked in. Mr. Morgan was perched on a stool, milking one of the three cows by hand.

Jayden ducked, but Mr. Morgan had glanced up and had seen him. Jayden gritted his teeth.

Mr. Morgan waved to him. "Come in, son. Come and see how it's done."

Jayden sighed. He had no choice. Wrinkling his nose at the smell of fresh cow dung, he carefully made his way to the stall where Mr. Morgan sat. Apart from the three cows, a large mother pig with numerous piglets also resided in the barn. He gagged at the stench. He should have given the barn a wide berth.

"Ever milked a cow?" Mr. Morgan looked up but continued squirting milk from the cow's teats into the metal bucket without missing a beat.

Jayden shook his head.

"It's not as hard as it looks. Would you like to try?"

Jayden crossed his arms, and angling his head, studied Mr. Morgan's action. It didn't look that hard. He shrugged. "Okay."

"Pull up a stool and I'll get you started."

Jayden grabbed a stool from the side and sat near Mr. Morgan. The cow seemed so much bigger now he was perched beside her. She turned her head as if she was checking him out.

"Her name's Betsy." Mr. Morgan gave her side a gentle rub.

Betsy turned her head back to the feed trough and resumed eating.

"It's not hard, you just need to get a rhythm going. Put your hand around the teat like this." Mr. Morgan squeezed the tips of his thumb and forefinger together, making a circle, before slipping his hand around one of Betsy's teats.

Jayden copied him, but just in the air.

"Then squeeze gently on the teat, pulling down at the same time. Like this."

He leaned forward and watched intently. It looked easy.

"Okay, your turn." Mr. Morgan grinned as he shifted to the side and motioned for Jayden to take his place.

Jayden hooked his feet around the legs of the stool, took a deep breath, and placed his hand around one of the cow's teats like he'd been shown. He wasn't expecting it to be so warm and firm. He glanced at Mr. Morgan and pulled a face. "It feels strange."

"I guess it does." Mr. Morgan laughed. "Okay, now squeeze gently and pull down."

Jayden did what he was told, but nothing came out. He tried again. Still nothing. "What am I doing wrong?" He glanced at Mr. Morgan.

"Nothing. Just get a rolling action going. Nice and steady. You'll get a feel for it."

Jayden drew another breath and started again. He could do this. How hard could it be? This time a squirt came out and he laughed.

"That's it, you've got it." Mr. Morgan patted him on the back. "You're a natural."

A proud grin grew on Jayden's face as the bucket began to fill.

"Now try both hands."

"Okay." Jayden shifted on the stool to get a better position, and then placed his right hand on one teat, getting that going before starting with his left hand. Mr. Morgan was right—it didn't take long to get a rhythm going.

"You're doing great."

Jayden's mouth curved into a smile, but when a flash of red hair caught his eye, he stiffened. Angie was watching him, but he didn't stop. He took some quick breaths and then focused on Betsy, but he couldn't help the occasional glance at Angie.

She stepped closer and crossed her arms as she leaned on a railing, an amused grin growing on her face. "Anyone would think you've done this before!"

"He's doing well, isn't he?" Mr. Morgan stood and leaned on the rail beside her.

"Yes, he is. A natural."

Jayden's heart swelled. Maybe he should go back to school and work towards becoming a vet sooner rather than later. But as an image of Tessa flashed through his mind, he lost his rhythm and the milk stopped flowing. He let out a heavy sigh and hung his head.

Mr. Morgan placed his hand on Jayden's shoulder. "It's okay, son. You did well. I can finish her off."

Jayden stood and moved aside, allowing Mr. Morgan to take over.

Angie held out her hand. Her face had grown serious. "Come for a walk?"

Jayden nodded and took her hand. Stepping out of the

barn, he sucked in the fresh air and tried to steady his thoughts.

"What's up?" Angie angled her head towards him.

He shrugged. "Just a lot going on in my head, that's all."

"Want to talk about it?"

"Maybe." He should tell Angie what he'd prayed last night. She'd understand. In fact, she'd be happy he was seeking God. But he wasn't quite ready.

They walked in silence for a good ten minutes. He didn't even know where they were heading, he just walked without taking notice of his surroundings, lost in thought. Inside him, everything was a jumble and his head felt like it was about to explode.

When they reached the edge of a small stream, Angie suggested they sit on a log.

Jayden stared at the crystal clear water flowing slowly downstream. In this lovely, peaceful place, he should have been relaxed and happy, but both his heart and mind were heavy. If only he could run away with Angie and hide from the world.

"Would it help to talk now?"

Jayden lifted his head and met Angie's gaze. Her eyes were soft and caring, just like her voice. He drew in a breath. Yes, it was time—he needed to talk. He nodded.

"God's working on you, I can sense it."

His heart pounded. "I... I told God last night I want to know Him, but I feel so mixed up."

A huge smile grew on her face. "That's wonderful. That's what's happening to you. God's working on you, but there's a battle going on inside you. Satan doesn't want to let God have you."

Jayden's brows puckered. "Is Satan real?"

Angie nodded, her expression growing serious. "You bet. There's a spiritual battle going on inside you right now. That's what it feels like, isn't it? A battleground?"

He nodded. That's exactly what it was like.

"If you ask Jesus into your life, you'll have God on your side, and he'll have won the battle." Angie paused, her gaze steady. "Would you like to do that?"

No, he wasn't ready. He still didn't know what it all meant. "I need to know more."

"That's okay, but don't put it off too long. You'll never know everything this side of heaven—at some stage you just have to ask God into your heart."

He tried to smile. "I won't. I promise."

LATER THAT MORNING, sitting in church beside Angie and her family, Jayden listened to the message with an open heart and allowed the words of the worship songs to minister to him. When Pastor Graham offered an altar call at the end of the service, his heart quickened. This was it. Like Angie said, he'd never know everything, but he knew enough. He knew in his heart that God was real, and that God loved him enough to send His only Son to die for him so that he could have new life. That's all he needed to know.

Drawing a slow breath, he stood and walked to the front. Tears streamed down his face, but he didn't care. He was giving his life to God, and from this day forward he'd live in the knowledge that he was loved by the Creator, cleansed, forgiven and guilt free. He'd face all that lay ahead of him with

God in his heart. God would lead and guide him, and give him direction.

He remained at the front doing business with God for a long time. Pastor Graham prayed with him, and Angie and her parents joined him. A weight lifted off his shoulders and his heart, and was replaced with a sense of freedom and joy he'd not experienced before. Today was the beginning of his new life.

"Congratulations, Jayden." Angie beamed at him as she gave him a huge hug. Her eyes were red, but her smile couldn't have been more genuine.

"Thank you. Thank you for everything." He gazed into her eyes. "I mean that, I really do. If I hadn't met you…"

She lifted her finger and placed it over his lips. "But you did. That's all that matters."

"Yes, and I'm so glad." He smiled at her before straightening. "You know what I need to do now?"

Angie shook her head.

"I need to call Dad."

CHAPTER 11

*B*en woke to the sound of the phone ringing. He glanced at the clock on his bedside table. *Five a.m.* He groaned.

Tessa stirred. "Are you going to get that?" Her voice was sleepy and slow.

"Yes…" Reaching over, he grabbed the phone and held it to his ear.

"Dad…"

Ben's eyes widened and he sat with a jolt. "Jayden… is it really you?"

"Yes, I'm… I'm so sorry, Dad." Jayden's voice choked. But it didn't sound like Jayden at all. His voice was deeper.

"It's okay. It's all okay." Ben suddenly felt light headed.

"Really?"

"Yes…"

Tessa slipped her arm around Ben's shoulder.

Jayden sniffled. "I've… I've got something to tell you."

Ben stiffened. His heart pounded. Was Jayden in trouble? Had something happened to Kathryn? "What is it, son? What's happened?" Ben could barely speak.

"It's okay, Dad. It's good news."

Ben let out a relieved sigh. "You had me concerned. What is it, then? Are you coming home?"

Silence.

"No… not yet…" Another pause. "I… I became a Christian today."

Ben blinked. "Really? That's wonderful." Tears streamed down his face. "Congratulations." He couldn't keep the excitement out of his voice.

"Thank you."

"That's even better news than telling us you're coming home." Ben laughed. "And that's saying something."

"I know." Another silence. "Dad, I'm so sorry. I don't know what I'm doing, but this is a start. Okay?"

"Okay." Ben gulped. "It's just fantastic to hear your voice. But you sound different."

"Yes, I'm all grown up."

"And you have a girlfriend."

"Yes. She's here with me now."

Ben winced. "She sounds like a nice girl."

"She is. The best."

Ben drew a slow breath. "And you're okay?"

"Yes." Jayden paused. "I need to go now, but I just wanted to give you my news."

"Thank you," Ben swallowed hard and pulled Tessa close. "Tessa and I appreciate it."

"I'll call again soon."

Ben squeezed his eyes, pushing his tears back. "We'll look forward to it."

"Bye, Dad."

"Good-bye Jayden. We love you."

BEN REPLACED the receiver and leaned against the pillows, stroking Tessa's hair as she rested her head on his chest. "I don't believe it, Tess. He rang. And he's a Christian." His voice broke again as happy tears stung his eyes.

Tessa hugged him and lifted her head. "It's the best news. It's what we've been praying for."

He nodded. Grabbing a tissue, he wiped his face and blew his nose. "I know. I'm still pinching myself." Moments passed. A million thoughts flashed through his mind. How did it happen? Where was Jayden when he called? Where was he when he gave his heart to the Lord? A tinge of sadness settled on Ben's heart. He shouldn't be sad, but how could he not be? Jayden had grown up so much, and he and Tess were missing out on so much of his life. But maybe God had used everything to bring him to this point. They needed to rejoice and be happy for him. And as Jayden said, it was a start.

Ben straightened and turned to Tessa. "We need to pray, Tess. To thank God."

Tessa struggled to sit. "Yes, we do."

He held her hand and bowed his head. He was still struggling to believe what had just happened. It was truly amazing, almost unbelievable. He cleared his throat and sucked in a breath. "Lord, I don't really know what to say, apart from 'thank You'. Thank You that Jayden called, and thank You for answering our prayers." He paused, swallowing hard. "Thank You for not giving up on him, dear Lord. This is just the best news." He paused again. "Be with Jayden in the days ahead. Help him to grow in You, and to become the young man You want him to be. And Lord, we still ask You to bring him home, but in Your time, not ours. In Jesus' precious name we pray, Amen." Ben squeezed his eyes shut as an overwhelming sense of joy and expectation filled his heart.

Tessa sniffed as she squeezed his hand. "Amen." She straightened further, wiping her eyes with her fingers. "This is just so exciting. I don't know how I'm going to concentrate at work today."

Ben chuckled as he met her gaze. "Me either."

She slid out of bed and threw on her dressing gown, doing the tie up loosely over her tummy. "I need to tell Mum and Dad. And Margaret. And Stephanie. And Fraser, and…"

Ben's head shot up. "Whoa, Tess, slow down. We don't want the baby to come yet."

"I've still got ages to go. I'm fine."

"Yes, but you know what the doctor said."

Tessa paused, stepping closer to him and reaching out her hand. "It's okay. I'm perfectly fine."

"I'm sorry, I just get a little anxious when I see you overly excited, that's all."

"I understand. We both want this baby to come with no problems. And it will." Her smile broadened as she placed his hand on her tummy.

He relaxed when the baby moved. There was nothing better. Well, apart from Jayden calling. His heart warmed as Tessa leaned forward and placed a kiss on his forehead.

CHAPTER 11 | 95

"I'm off to make those calls." She flashed him a smile that lit up her face. She turned to leave, but then stopped and spun around. "We should celebrate. Ask everybody over."

Ben drew his brows together. "We only just saw everyone."

She chuckled. "I don't think they'll mind getting together again for such a special occasion."

He angled his head. "What are you thinking?"

"Dinner here tonight?" She raised a brow.

"We're becoming quite the entertainers!"

"And you're loving it!" And with that, she leaned forward and gave him another kiss, this time on his lips. He held his breath as she sashayed awkwardly out of the room towards the steps, silently praying she'd make it safely.

TESSA HUNG up the phone after making her calls and flopped onto the couch. It was exhausting work talking to so many people one after the other. Luckily, none of them had minded being woken so early. She picked up the mug of coffee Ben had placed beside her almost half an hour ago and took a sip. *Ugh! Luke warm.* Never mind, she'd make a fresh brew shortly.

The sky had lightened while she'd been on the phone. A new day was beginning, and what a day it was. It still seemed surreal. Jayden's news was beyond their wildest dreams, but the fact he had a girlfriend concerned her. Would he be prepared to leave her and come home? Surely he was too young to be serious. *But was he?* Tessa's thoughts drifted back to the heady days when she and Michael had started dating. She'd only been seventeen, but even after dating for only a month, she was convinced she couldn't live without him. Young love. So sweet. So hard to let go. She took another sip of her cold coffee. Jayden would be torn, no doubt about it. *Just another thing to pray for.*

Bindy and Sparky sprang up from their mats as Ben reappeared, showered and dressed for the day, and began wagging their tails at him.

"I thought we could take a walk this morning." Tessa sat forward and drained her coffee, pulling a face as the cold liquid slid down her throat.

Ben glanced at his watch. "Guess I could fit a quick one in."

"You don't need to be at work for another two hours!"

"I know, but I'll need to be home earlier than normal tonight."

"Yes, you do." She inched herself off the couch and walked towards him, one hand on the small of her back. What would it be like when she was nine months? Everyone told her she already looked like a bean pole with a ball out front, but she actually felt like a cow. Not surprising really, given the amount of chocolate she was eating. She sidled up to him and wrapped her arms around him, all the while trying to ignore the dogs as she gazed into his eyes. "It'd be nice to go for a short walk together, wouldn't it?"

Ben placed his hands on her waist and smiled down at her. "Yes, it would." He lowered his head and kissed her. "Let's go. Otherwise I'll be tempted to go back to bed."

"Ben! You know what the doctor said!"

His face fell. "Yes, I do. Come on then, let's go." He dropped his hands and stepped into the utility room, returning a second later with the dogs' leashes.

Bindy and Sparky sat on command and waited while he clipped their leashes on. He glanced up. "Sure you're okay to do this?"

She rolled her eyes. "Yes, Ben. I'm up to this."

He raised a brow as his eyes ran down the length of her body. "Going out like that?"

Tessa glanced down at her attire and laughed. "No. Let me get dressed." She stepped into the downstairs' bathroom and quickly changed into her walking clothes, and in less than a minute joined Ben and the dogs outside.

ALL DAY AT WORK, Tessa hummed worship songs. She still had to pinch herself that after almost a year of praying, Jayden had finally called. It truly was unbelievable. She couldn't wait to tell Harrison. He'd be so happy that Jayden hadn't waited as long as he had to contact his parents.

Tessa invited him and his fiancée, Zoe, to the celebration, but they had other plans and had to decline.

Dinner that night was a happy occasion, ending in a worship and prayer time in Ben and Tessa's living room. After everyone left, Ben wrapped his arms around her and pulled her tight. He nuzzled her neck, sending tingles down her body.

"Ben! We need to clean up."

"It can wait."

She let out a small laugh as she relaxed in his arms.

CHAPTER 12

One day a few weeks later, Jayden was about to leave work when he spotted Mom standing outside on the pavement. Even though a scarf sat high on her neck, almost covering her face, he was sure it was her. He released a huge sigh. Especially now he was a Christian, he knew he should have more compassion, but every time he saw her, he had to work hard to hide his frustration.

Mom had blinders on as far as Buck was concerned. Everyone else could see what was happening to her. How could she be so stupid? Sighing heavily again, Jayden grabbed his jacket and slipped it on, all the while praying for patience.

As he stepped outside, a gust of wind caught his cap and blew it off, sending it flying into the air. He rushed after it, retrieved it, and stuck it firmly back on his head. When he turned around, Mom was gone. He looked both ways, and then walked up and down the street, but there was no sign of her.

He shrugged and headed towards home. He really should get his bike fixed.

When he reached his apartment, he grabbed a frozen meal out of the freezer and placed it into the microwave, then picked up his guitar to practice for the weekend. He was playing in a band with Gareth, Angie and Dave at a youth camp this weekend, but still had a lot to learn.

The microwave dinged. He put his guitar down and pulled out his meal of macaroni and cheese, squeezed almost half a bottle of ketchup over it, and sitting down, flicked the television on. He choked on his first mouthful. A picture of Mom was on the television with a *'Breaking News'* headline running across the screen. He turned up the volume and leaned forward. The image changed to one of Buck, and of the cottage he and Mom shared, cordoned off with Police tape.

A female reporter stood outside the cottage, speaking in a serious voice. "The body of William Buckley, commonly known as Buck, was found early this afternoon when one of his co-workers checked on him after Mr. Buckley failed to turn up for work. The Police are currently seeking any information on the whereabouts of his partner, Kathryn Middleton. They would like to question her about the incident."

Jayden gulped. *Has Mom killed Buck? Surely not.* His stomach lurched. He raced for the bathroom and spewed up the contents of his stomach. His chest heaved. How could this have happened? As much as she frustrated him, she was still his mother. Buck must have driven her to it.

The faint ringing of his cell phone reached Jayden's ears. He wiped his mouth and sprinted to the kitchen, picking up his phone. *Angie.* He sucked in a quick breath and answered.

"Angie... you heard?"

"Yes. We can't believe it. Are you okay, Jayden?"

Jayden slumped against the wall. Was he okay? No, he wasn't. His stomach felt like it didn't belong to him, and his head spun like a top. He slithered onto the floor, holding his head in his hand. "No, I'm not okay."

"Stay there. Dad said we'll be there as soon as we can."

"Okay." Jayden could barely speak. He ended the call and put the phone down. A different story was on the television screen. Had he imagined it? No, Angie had called, and she and her dad were on the way over. He straightened. Maybe that's why Mom disappeared—maybe she'd just wanted to see him once more. If only his cap hadn't blown off.

He leaned forward, put his elbows on his knees and his hands over his head. He needed to settle his thoughts before Angie and Mr. Morgan arrived. He drew a slow breath and held it. The noise from the television faded into the background as he began to pray. With no real idea of what to ask for, he just asked God to keep her safe, wherever she might be.

He looked up when a soft knock sounded on the door a short while later. When he opened it, Angie held out her arms to him. Her eyes blurred with tears as he stepped forward. He didn't cry. He just clung to her, his body numb.

"Come and sit." Angie led him to the sofa. Mr. Morgan followed, placing his hand gently on his back.

Angie's face was white, and so serious. Jayden had never seen her like this. But they'd never had a murder before.

"Dad made some calls on our way over, and the Police will be here any minute. They want to talk to you about your mother." Her voice was quiet and steady. Controlled.

Jayden sucked in another breath. He'd have to tell the Police he'd seen her.

Within seconds another knock, this time louder and firmer, sounded on the door. Mr. Morgan rose and answered it. Two officers in uniform entered, introducing themselves as Officers Wallace and Brown. Officer Wallace, the older of the two, led the conversation as they sat around Jayden's small kitchen table. Angie sat beside Jayden, holding his hand. Mr. Morgan stood to the side with his arms folded.

"Jayden, we're investigating the murder of William Buckley, commonly known as Buck. We believe your mother was living with him?"

Jayden nodded.

"Can you tell us the last time you saw your mother?"

Jayden gulped. He couldn't lie to them. He looked down before slowly lifting his gaze. "I... I thought I saw her outside the shop this afternoon." He cleared his throat and straightened. "I work at the Value Village Thrift store in town. She sometimes walks past there and waits for me to finish work, but this afternoon, my cap blew off and I chased it, and when I looked for her, she wasn't there."

"Are you sure it was her?" The officer's gaze was fixed on Jayden.

Jayden shrugged. "I think it was her, but I can't be sure."

"What was she wearing?"

He tried to think. All he could really remember was the scarf. "I know she was wearing a scarf. She had it up around her head, and it was some kind of green color. Other than that, I'm not sure. Like I said, I only caught a glimpse of her through the window before she disappeared."

Officer Brown made some notes.

"Before today, when was the last time you saw her?" Officer Wallace asked.

Jayden sighed, his shoulders slumping. "Just over three weeks ago. On my birthday. She came by and we had breakfast together."

"Is it strange you haven't seen her since then?"

Jayden tilted his head. He'd been so busy with church activities since then he hadn't taken that much notice. Mom just seemed to pop in and out of his life whenever it suited her, or to be honest, when she wanted something. *Usually money.* But yes, it was kind of strange he hadn't seen her since then. Jayden felt the color drain from his face. *Maybe Mom didn't kill Buck. Maybe she's been dead all this time.*

"Do you mind if we take a look around?"

Jayden blinked. "She's not here, if that's what you're thinking. There's nowhere for her to hide, but go ahead."

"Thanks, son. We will."

Officer Brown stood and walked around the studio apartment, picking up things here and there before putting them back down, including the photo of Bindy and Sparky Dad had sent him for his birthday.

"Aren't you a bit young to be living on your own?" Officer Wallace narrowed his eyes. "And you're not from around here."

Jayden squirmed under the officer's steady gaze. *Here goes. He's going to deport me.*

Mr. Morgan stepped forward and placed his hand on Jayden's shoulder. "I don't see what that has to do with anything, Tom."

"Just making an observation, Robert, that's all." Officer Wallace glanced up and met Mr. Morgan's gaze.

"He's a good boy. Just had a hard time, that's all."

Officer Wallace returned his focus to Jayden. "Do you have any idea where your mother might have gone? Her car's missing."

Jayden shook his head. "I have no idea."

The officer stood. "Right, if you hear from her, make sure you contact us immediately."

"Yes, sir. I will."

"Thanks for your time." The officers nodded, shook Mr. Morgan's hand, and then exited the apartment.

When the door shut behind them, Jayden let out a huge breath and flopped his head onto his folded arms.

Angie rubbed his back. "Are you okay?"

He raised his head slowly and turned to face her. Tears clouded his vision before they rolled down his cheeks. She pulled him close and hugged him.

Mr. Morgan sat down. "We're here for you, son."

Jayden nodded, swallowing hard. He lifted his head off Angie's shoulder and wiped his face with his sleeve before turning to face Mr. Morgan. "Thank you."

"Come home with us. You can't stay here alone."

"What if Mom tries to find me?"

"We'll let your neighbors know. You'll be better off with company."

Mr. Morgan was right. How could he stay here on his own? He'd go crazy. "Okay. Thank you."

"Grab an overnight bag and we'll go."

It didn't take Jayden long to throw a few clothes into a bag, and within minutes he was sitting in the front seat of Mr. Morgan's SUV. Angie sat in the seat behind him. He kept his eyes peeled for his mother or her car, but in the semi darkness, it was difficult to make out anything. Several times he thought he saw her, only to realize it was someone totally different. Besides, he had this horrible tightness in his chest. He had a feeling she was dead.

KATHRYN HAD TO PULL OVER—SHE'D been struggling to stay awake for goodness knows how long. If only she hadn't taken those tablets. She leaned forward over the steering wheel. Everything was double, and her head spun. She glanced in the rear vision mirror. No one was following. But she needed to keep driving. A sudden chill ran through her body. *Buck would be dead by now.*

But it was no good. She couldn't stay awake. Slowing down, she turned into a small side road and drove a short distance until the car was hidden from the main road. She turned off the engine and slumped in her seat.

CHAPTER 13

Mrs. Morgan rushed out of the house as Mr. Morgan's SUV came to a halt just outside the shed. When Jayden climbed out of the car, she drew him into a hug, rubbing his back as she pulled him close.

Jayden squeezed his eyes closed, forcing himself not to break down. If only his mother had been like Mrs. Morgan.

Moments passed. She finally released him. Glancing at her husband, she placed her arm around Jayden's shoulders and walked him inside.

"I've made some hot chocolate. Take a seat and I'll pour you a mug." She filled two mugs of the hot drink from the saucepan sitting on her large stove and placed them in front of him and Angie. "You must be in shock. Can I get you anything else?"

Jayden shook his head. "No, I couldn't eat anything, but thank you." He tried to smile, but couldn't.

"I understand." Her voice was so quiet and caring as she rubbed his shoulder. "It must be terrible for you."

Jayden looked up and met her soft eyes. All he could do was nod. His eyes watered, and all of a sudden, tears spilled down his cheeks. He buried his head in his hands and sobbed as a heavy sadness grabbed his heart. How had his life gotten into such a mess?

Mrs. Morgan pulled him close and rubbed his back. "There, there, let it out. It's okay."

Jayden didn't want to cry, but he couldn't stop. His heart ached with all the hurt he'd carried for so many years. He sobbed into Mrs. Morgan's chest until he had no more sobs left.

"It's okay, cry as much as you want. You don't need to be embarrassed, son." Mr. Morgan's strong, steady voice almost started him off again. Instead, Jayden sucked in a breath, his body shuddering as he fought to gain control. He slowly straightened and wiped his face with a tissue from the box Angie handed him.

"I'm sorry." Jayden gulped, his gaze traveling quickly between the three of them. "It all just got to me." He wiped his eyes again.

"We're not surprised, son. You've had a lot to deal with." Mr. Morgan rubbed his chin. "When you're up to it, we should have a good talk about everything. But only when you're ready."

Jayden nodded. "That would be good, thank you." He sucked in a breath and gulped. "I should call Dad."

Mr. Morgan nodded. "Only if you're up to it, otherwise I can call."

Was he up to it? Could he speak to Dad on the phone and

not break down? Jayden inhaled slowly. Yes, he could. *He would.* "Yes, I can do it."

"Okay, we'll be in the next room if you need us."

"Thank you."

"Would you like me to stay?" Angie asked with a soft voice as she touched his hand lightly.

He shifted his gaze to her and nodded.

She squeezed his hand.

After her parents left the room, Jayden steeled himself and dialed Dad's number.

Angie held his gaze as the phone rang.

His heart thumped. Seconds passed. When Dad answered, Jayden's lip quivered. He couldn't speak.

"Jayden… is that you?"

"Yes, Dad, it's me." Jayden spoke quietly.

"What's wrong, son?"

Jayden gulped. "It's Mom. The police think she's killed someone."

For a long moment, Dad didn't say anything.

"What… what makes them think that?"

"The man she's been living with has been murdered. The police think she did it."

"Have they charged her?"

"No, they don't know where she is."

Silence.

"Are they looking for anyone else?"

Jayden drew in a breath. "Not that I know of."

"Where are you?"

"At Angie's place."

"Would you like me to come over? I can jump on a plane right now."

Jayden's head whirled. "Ah… I don't know. It's only just happened. Let me think about that, okay?"

"All right, but I can come straight away if you want."

Tears pricked Jayden's eyes as a lump formed in his throat. "Thanks Dad. I'll let you know."

"No problem. How are you holding up? Are you okay?"

Jayden drew a breath. Was he all right? Not really, but he couldn't have asked for better people to be with. "Kind of. Angie's parents have been really good."

"I'm pleased to hear that." There was a hint of sadness in Dad's voice.

"I love you, Dad." Jayden's voice caught.

"I love you too, son."

"I'll call again soon." Jayden's voice was no more than a whisper.

"We'll be praying for you."

"Thanks." Jayden could barely get the last word out before he hung up.

Angie squeezed his hand and sat quietly.

Should he ask Dad to come? Jayden's head whirled. Everything would be different if he did.

"You okay?" Angie leaned forward and tilted his chin with her finger. The concern in her eyes just made him love her more.

Blinking back tears, Jayden shook his head.

"What's up?" Angie tilted his head up again.

He met her gaze. A feeling that everything was about to change settled heavily on his heart. Squeezing her hand, his gaze traveled over her face. He loved every bit of her, from the curls of red hair that spiraled down her neck, to her green eyes that sparkled like emeralds, and to her smile that made him feel all warm and fuzzy inside. There was nothing he didn't love about Angie Morgan.

But he didn't deserve someone as loving and kind as her. It was amazing that her parents allowed her to date him. They probably wouldn't now, not with a murderer as a mother. But the Morgan's weren't like that. The way they'd accepted Jessica's pregnancy, even though they were saddened by it, they hadn't disowned her like Blake's parents had disowned him. They loved and accepted everyone, and everyone loved them. If only all families were like that. Not messed up like his.

He blinked. Angie was waiting for an answer. He drew a slow breath. "Just thinking."

She gave him a wistful smile. "There's a lot to think about."

Yes, there was. He ran his hand over his head. "I think I need that talk."

Angie nodded. "Good idea."

She leaned forward and kissed his cheek before standing and walking with him into the living room where her parents were seated on a sofa, chatting quietly. Jessica and Simon were engrossed in a game of chess, but looked up as Angie and Jayden entered the room.

"How did it go?" Concern was written all over Mrs. Morgan's face.

Jayden's shoulders slumped. "Dad was shocked." He paused. Should he tell them that Dad had offered to come over? He glanced at Angie and sighed. *He probably should.* "He offered to come over."

Mrs. Morgan's eyes misted over. "Oh, Jayden, that's lovely of him. What a thoughtful man."

Jayden gulped. Maybe he should have told Dad to come.

"What did you say?" Mr. Morgan asked.

Jayden shuffled his feet before answering. "I told him I'd think about it."

"I can understand that." Mr. Morgan patted the seat opposite him. "Come and sit."

Jayden glanced at Angie and then led her to the sofa opposite her parents. It was time to come clean about everything.

"We'd like to pray for your mom. Is that okay?" Mr. Morgan straightened in his seat and leaned forward a little.

Jayden nodded.

Angie squeezed his hand and shifted closer.

"Jess, Simon, come and join us." Mrs. Morgan held her hand out to the two of them.

They raised their brows at each other before they stood and moved closer, joining their parents and Angie and Jayden.

"We've got some serious stuff going on here." Mr. Morgan's gaze traveled around his family. "Stuff you'd hope no one would ever have to deal with, but it's happened, and we have no idea how it's going to end. We need to support Jayden. And we have to ask God to help us through it. Okay?"

Everyone nodded. Mr. Morgan reached out and placed his hand on Jayden's shoulder. The others joined hands.

"Let's pray." Mr. Morgan began. "Dear Heavenly Father, we come to You with heavy hearts. Never in our wildest dreams would we have thought that anything like this could happen, and we're still in shock. Lord, we pray for Jayden's mother, wherever she might be, that she might feel Your presence with her, even if she doesn't know You. Lord, we don't know what drove her to do this, if indeed she did do it, but Lord, we know she's a troubled woman, and that she's made plenty of bad choices, but Lord, we know that You still love her, regardless of what she's done, just like You love all of us, regardless of what we've done. None of us deserve Your favor, Lord, and we don't judge her. We just pray that somehow You can bring good out of this most horrible of situations.

"And Lord, we bring Jayden before you. Thank You that he's chosen to live for You, but Lord, we know he's carrying a lot of hurt, and we pray that You'll touch him deep inside and bring healing to his life. We pray that You'll help him see life through Your eyes, Lord, and that he'll learn to forgive, and to let go of things that might hold him back. We pray that he'll know true love in his life. Love that only comes from You, dear Lord. True love that never fails, and never disappoints."

Jayden brushed tears from his eyes.

Mr. Morgan continued. "And Lord, we pray for this dear little baby boy that Jessica's carrying. We know he wasn't planned, but we love him already, just as you do. Bless him, dear Lord, and help Jessica and Blake to work through everything that's ahead of them in the days, weeks and months ahead. We know it won't be easy, but we pray they'll put You first, and that they'll honor You in all they do. We ask all these things in Jesus' precious name, Amen."

Everyone sat quietly as a sense of God's presence filled their hearts. Tears rolled down Jayden's cheeks. Despite all the turmoil in his life, he had peace. He had no idea what would unfold, but God would see him through, and would show him the way. Of that he was certain.

CHAPTER 14

The first thing Jayden needed to do was to come clean. Mrs. Morgan had quickly prepared a supper of soup and toast, and everyone was sitting around the kitchen table. Mr. Morgan called the Police for any updates, but they had none—they were still searching for Ms. Middleton and would be in touch when they had any news.

Jayden inhaled and steeled himself. He glanced at Angie, and then cleared his throat. "I've... I've got something I need to say."

All eyes turned towards him.

"What is it, son?" Mr. Morgan asked as he glanced up from the toast he was buttering.

Jayden clenched his hands together to stop them shaking and gulped. "I haven't been completely honest with you all, and I need to. While we were praying, it was like God was telling me I needed to come clean, so that's what I'm doing."

Angie's eyes widened.

What must she be thinking? His stomach lurched. *Oh God, please don't let me lose her.*

"You'd better tell us, son, but I can't imagine it's that bad."

Jayden drew another breath and sighed. "You'll have to decide that once you hear." He fixed his gaze on his soup bowl for a second before raising his head. His heart pounded, but he needed to get it over with. His gaze shifted to Angie. "To start with, I'm not seventeen. I've just turned sixteen." Her eyes widened further. His heart fell. He'd lost her, he knew it. He turned his gaze back to the soup bowl and took another breath. "And this is the big one—I've overstayed, so I'm actually illegal." He paused, waiting for his words to sink in. "I... I didn't know to start with, but Mom wasn't able to get me a visa, and so she organized fake ID for me." He lifted his head and met Mr. Morgan's gaze. Mr. Morgan's expression hadn't changed. Jayden had no idea what he was thinking. "I didn't want to use it, but it got too complicated," he shifted his gaze to Angie, "and then when I got the job at the shop, I had to give my boss something, so I used it. I knew at some stage I'd get into trouble, but I didn't know what to do, so I just left it. Until now."

His shoulders slumped as he lowered his head. No one said anything. He'd shocked them. His hands shook and a lump settled in his stomach. He shouldn't have said anything, but he'd had no choice. It was the right thing to do—he couldn't ignore his conscience any longer.

Angie squeezed his hand.

He turned his head.

Her eyes brimmed with tears.

His heart burned. Nothing would ever be the same.

The tick of the clock on the far wall was the only sound he could hear above the ringing in his ears. Mrs. Morgan stood and wrapped her arms around him. Angie gripped his hand as tears streamed down her cheeks. Mr. Morgan remained seated but placed his hand on his shoulder.

Mr. Morgan was the first one to speak. "Thank you for telling us, son. It couldn't have been easy."

Jayden sucked in a breath as he turned his head, meeting Mr. Morgan's gaze. "No, it wasn't. I'm so sorry." He swallowed hard.

Mr. Morgan's brow inched lower. "As you said, it would have come out eventually. No need to do anything tonight. Let's sleep on it, and we'll pray about it. God will have a plan, I'm sure of it. He'll honor your obedience, son."

Jayden's heart quickened. He'd almost forgotten that God was on his side. He didn't have to handle this alone.

He managed a weak smile. "Thank you. I'm not sure how I'm going to sleep tonight, though."

"I can understand that. We can stay up all night if you like."

Mrs. Morgan placed her hand on Mr. Morgan's back. "Robert, the boy should get some sleep. We don't know what tomorrow will hold."

"That's true, but could you sleep if your mother was missing?"

"I guess I wouldn't. Okay then, we'll all stay up, for a while at least."

Everyone stiffened when the phone rang.

Jayden's heart pounded. Had they found Mom?

Mr. Morgan stood and lifted the phone from its cradle on the wall.

Jayden fixed his gaze on him. Mr. Morgan's expression didn't change; he was giving nothing away.

"Thank you, Officer. I'll bring him in."

Jayden's eyes widened. They must have found her. *But was she dead or alive?*

Mr. Morgan hung up the phone and returned to the table, but remained standing. "The Highway Patrol found your mother, Jayden. She's been taken in for questioning."

Jayden let out a huge sigh of relief.

"I told them I'll bring you in. Grab whatever you need and we'll go now."

"Can I come too?" Angie asked quietly.

"It's a school night, Angela." Mr. Morgan's voice grew firmer.

"How can I go to school?"

"You're right, I'm sorry. Yes, you can come." Mr. Morgan stepped towards Mrs. Morgan and kissed her tenderly on the cheek. "I'll call."

"I'll be praying for you all." Mrs. Morgan looked into her husband's eyes before turning her attention to Jayden. She reached out and squeezed his arm. "And I'll be praying for your mom."

"Thank you." It was all he could manage.

The drive into town was made in silence. Jayden was lost in his thoughts, almost unaware it had begun to rain until Mr. Morgan hit a puddle and a huge splash of water landed on his window. He blinked and straightened in his seat beside Mr. Morgan.

"Are you okay?" Mr. Morgan glanced at him quickly.

Jayden drew a slow breath. "I think so. I knew something

would have to happen eventually. Mom was going from bad to worse, but she just couldn't see it."

"One thing I've learned is that you have no control over what others do with their lives. Everyone makes their decisions, good or bad, and they have to face the consequences. Sometimes people have to hit the bottom before they're prepared to look at themselves. And even then, only some are prepared to make changes. Most don't. You can't force anyone to do something they don't want to do. Even God doesn't do that."

"So what's the purpose of praying for them?"

"Our prayers are never in vain. As long as we keep praying, God will keep knocking. It's up to them if they answer the door or not."

THE HUNTERS HOLLOW Police Station was on the main road going through town, not far from the church Jayden had visited on his own last Christmas Eve, his first night in Hunters Hollow. How long ago that seemed now.

He'd passed the station many times on his bicycle but had never been inside. It was only small, and as he and Angie followed Mr. Morgan inside, he got the impression that Buck's murder was the biggest thing that had happened here in some time. The four plastic seats in the waiting area were empty. Understandable given it was close to midnight. The only poster pinned to the notice board, other than the several 'Missing Persons' ones, had Mom's photo on it.

A bell, with instructions to ring it should the desk be unmanned, sat on the front counter. Mr. Morgan rang it. The tingling sound echoed down the hallway, from where the sound of shoes squelching on the tiled floor reached Jayden's ears. The owner of those shoes, a short, round officer he hadn't seen before, appeared around the corner and punched numbers into a keypad to open the door to the front counter area.

"Ah, Mr. Morgan. And I assume this is Jayden." The officer's gaze flashed to him for a moment as he settled in behind the counter.

"Yes, Officer. This is Jayden, and my daughter, Angela."

"Thanks for coming in. Ms. Middleton is still being interviewed, so you'll need to wait out here, I'm afraid. There's a vending machine in the corner if you need anything to eat or drink, or I can get you some water. I don't know how long she'll be."

"I'd like to get her a lawyer, Officer."

"We're only talking with her at this stage, Mr. Morgan." The officer looked at Mr. Morgan over the top of his steel-rimmed glasses.

"Yes, but for her own benefit, I think she needs one now." Mr. Morgan leaned on the counter and lowered his voice. "Especially if you're looking at murder."

The officer sighed. "She hasn't asked for one."

"That's because she probably can't afford one. I'll make some calls—I'll cover the cost."

Jayden's eyes widened. *Mr. Morgan would do that for Mom?*

"All right, if you need to. We'll stop questioning until morning, but we'll hold her overnight."

"Can we see her?"

"Follow me."

Jayden's heart pounded as he stood and followed the officer and Mr. Morgan through the door, down the hallway, and into an interview room.

Jayden gasped. Mom's eyes seemed empty; her cheeks were sunken and her skin sallow. What had happened in the few weeks since he'd seen her last? If only he'd made more of an effort to see her, to look after her. But then, he recalled Mr. Morgan's words: *'We can't control what choices people make.'* How many times had he pleaded with her to leave Buck? She just wouldn't listen.

Mom looked up as he took a seat opposite her. She held out her hand, willing him to take it. Her nails, broken and jagged, were a far cry from the highly manicured nails she used to be so proud of. Her eyes pleaded with him. "I didn't do it, Jay." She sounded so pitiful. It barely sounded like her.

Jayden held her gaze as a mixture of emotions welled up inside him. He began to seethe. She looked so pathetic. He swallowed hard. He shouldn't be feeling this way. God would be disappointed. But she'd been so stupid. He pinned her with his eyes. "Why didn't you leave him, Mom?" He tried hard not to spit the words.

Tears welled in her eyes. "I tried, Jay, but I couldn't."

"Why not?"

She hung her head and sobbed. "The drugs. I… I can't do without them."

Jayden leaned back in his chair and folded his arms. "You're going to have to now."

She lifted her head. "But I didn't kill him. You have to believe me. I didn't do it." She broke down in tears and lowered her head onto her arms as she sobbed.

Jayden narrowed his eyes and studied her. "Then tell me what happened."

The officer stepped forward. "Time's up, I'm afraid. You'll have to come back tomorrow."

"We'll get you a lawyer, Kathryn." Mr. Morgan said as he stood.

Tears streamed down her face as she reached out for Jayden. "Don't leave me here, Jay."

"We have no choice." Jayden stood watching as the officer supported her as he led her away. A lump grew in his throat. How would she survive the night in a cold, damp cell?

CHAPTER 15

*J*ayden couldn't get Mom out of his head. How had she fallen so low? He tossed in his bed. Squeezing his eyes shut, he tried desperately to clear his mind so he could sleep. But other thoughts bombarded him. What was going to happen now the Morgan's knew he'd overstayed? How much more time did he have with Angie? And what if Dad decided to come? The sheets grew damp from his sweat. After tossing and turning for more than an hour, he threw the covers off and sat up before pelting a pillow at the wall and clenching his jaw. If only he could yell.

Tears streamed down his face, his breaths coming hard and fast. Where was God when he needed Him? Jayden sucked in a long breath and let it out slowly. Eventually he calmed. The Bible sitting on the bedside table caught his attention. His shoulders slumped as he glanced heavenward. *God, if You're really on my side, I need to hear from You now.* He reached for the Bible and flipped it open to 1 Peter 5:7, one of the verses Angie suggested he memorize. He read the verse aloud: *"Cast all your anxiety on Him because He cares for you."* Yeah, right. *Do you really care, God?* He re-read the verse and continued on.

As he continued reading, his heart calmed, and assurance that God really did care grew within him. He didn't need to be anxious because God, the Creator of the universe, was on his side, and somehow it would all work out. Even if his mother was a murderer and he was illegal.

He closed his eyes and prayed. He prayed for himself, for Mom, for Dad and Tessa, for what was going to happen with him being illegal, and with Angie. As he prayed, a strength he couldn't explain coursed through his body, and he knew beyond a shadow of a doubt that whatever happened, he'd survive. God was with him.

As the first sign of daylight peeked through the bedroom window, Jayden finally slept.

BETHANY MORGAN SAT at the kitchen table in her bathrobe, cradling a steaming mug of coffee between her hands. She lifted her gaze and looked at her husband. "What's going to happen, Robert?"

Her husband ran his hand through his hair and sighed. "I don't know. It seems cut and dried, but you never know. She's saying she didn't do it."

"Do you believe her?" she asked quietly.

He drew a slow breath and held her gaze. "Somehow I do. I think she's telling the truth."

"Well, hopefully a lawyer will get her off if that's the case."

"I have a feeling the Police will find something that proves she didn't do it."

Bethany reached out and squeezed Robert's hand. "I hope you're right."

"So do I. For Jayden's sake."

"What's going to happen to him? Will they send him home?"

Robert nodded. "I'd say so."

She winced. "Angie will be devastated."

Sighing, Robert leaned back in his chair. "I know. But I think it's time for him to go home to his family." He tapped his fingers on the table. "In fact, I was thinking of calling his dad and having a chat."

"That's a wonderful idea. I can't imagine how they're feeling."

Robert glanced at his watch and straightened. "I'll call now."

As he picked up the phone, Jessica entered the kitchen. Her eyes were red and swollen.

Bethany reached out and gently pulled her onto her lap, wrapping her arms around her. "What's wrong, sweetheart?"

Tears welled in her eyes. She sucked in a breath as a shudder ran through her body. "Blake called. We've broken up." She sobbed. "He doesn't want to be with me anymore."

Bethany held her daughter tightly and closed her eyes. She and Robert had both known this day would come, but they hadn't expected it so soon. How could Blake do this to her now?

She pulled Jessica closer and rocked her like a baby. "You'll be all right, sweetheart. We're here for you." She rested her head on top of Jessica's and met Robert's gaze. *Two daughters. Two broken hearts.*

JAYDEN WOKE to a knock on his door. He sat with a start and glanced at the clock. *Midday already.* How had he slept so long? He wiped the sleep from his eyes and looked around. Why was he here and not in his own bed? Then it all came back. Mom had killed Buck, and he'd confessed to Angie and her parents. He began to hyperventilate, but then controlled himself. It would be okay. *Everything would be okay.* God was with him. He slipped out of bed and into his jeans before opening the door.

Mr. Morgan stood in the doorway, Angie beside him. The sparkle had returned to her eyes. His heart leaped. Did they have good news?

"Jayden, guess what?" Angie's voice had a trill to it.

"What?" Jayden's heart beat faster.

A broad smile grew on her face as she jiggled up and down on the spot. "They've let your mother go."

Jayden's eyes widened. "Really? How? Why?" His gaze traveled between Angie and her dad.

"She described the man she believed killed him. The police checked her story out, and they've let her go." Angie threw her arms around him.

Mr. Morgan cleared his throat. "Seems Buck told her to get away as quickly as she could, but he stayed, and got himself killed."

"So who did it?" Jayden's brows came together.

Mr. Morgan sighed. "One of the drug dealers in town. Did you know your mother was mixed up with them?"

Jayden's shoulders slumped. "I didn't know for sure, but I knew something was different." He looked up. "Where is she now?"

"They've taken her to the hospital. They'll keep her in for a while."

Jayden nodded slowly. "Can I see her?"

"Best to wait a while. She's not in a good way at the moment."

Jayden's mind raced. If Buck was no longer around, and she got off the drugs, she could come and live with him and they could start all over again. *Except for one little detail.* He would probably get deported any day. Mom could stay—she had a long-term visa, thanks to Luke Emerson. *But maybe she'll choose to come home.* Jayden's chest tightened. He didn't want to leave Angie.

"Come and have something to eat. Lunch is almost ready."

Angie took his hand and walked beside him to the kitchen where her mother was slicing bread. He felt dazed. Everything seemed surreal. But his stomach rumbled at the smell of freshly baked bread.

Mrs. Morgan flashed him a warm smile. "Good news about your mother."

He tried to return her smile, but didn't do a great job of it. "Yes, it is." He blinked. "It mustn't have been her I saw outside the shop yesterday."

Mrs. Morgan stopped slicing and angled her head. "No, it mustn't have been."

Jayden took a seat, but immediately stood again. "I need to call Dad and let him know."

"No need, son. I called him as soon as we found out." Mr. Morgan took a seat on the opposite side of the table. "So that's one matter dealt with. Well, almost…" He looked up and met Jayden's gaze. "There's a Rehab place run by a Christian organisation not far from here. We're going to suggest your mother goes there when she's released from the hospital."

Jayden sat back down. "I doubt she'd go. She's not into anything Christian."

"You might be surprised. I don't see she has many options."

"You've got a point, especially if I'm…" Jayden gulped and lowered his head. He couldn't say it.

"That's the next issue." Mrs. Morgan sat beside him and gently touched his wrist. "We wanted to talk to you about that."

A cold chill flowed down his spine.

"We're not going to tell the authorities. Mr. Morgan and I have prayed about it, and we believe you'll come to the right decision yourself, in your own time."

Was he hearing right? They weren't going to tell the Police? He could stay, at least for now? He reached for Angie's hand under the table and squeezed it. He turned his head and looked into her eyes which were brimming with tears.

"We don't condone it, Jayden, but we don't think it's our place to force things." Mr. Morgan looked at him with a serious expression from across the table.

"But shouldn't you tell them? Won't you get into trouble if you don't?"

"That's our decision, not yours. Don't you worry about that."

Jayden leaned back in his seat and crossed his arms. "So what you're saying is that I can stay, that you won't tell, and it's up to me to decide what to do?"

"That's pretty much it. We know how hard it's going to be for you, but we also believe that God will help you make the right decision at the right time, and that He'll give you the strength to do it, as long as you're trusting Him."

So no, they weren't saying he could stay; they were saying he should be the one to make the decision to do the right thing. "I'll be thrown into prison, though, won't I?"

Mr. Morgan laughed. "I don't think so. Not if you choose to go home. There may be some penalty, but I don't think they'll throw you into jail."

For a brief moment Jayden's body relaxed, but then tensed again. If he decided to go home, it would be without Angie.

CHAPTER 16

*J*ayden stayed with the Morgan's for the rest of the week—there was no way he could go back to work. Angie also took time off school, and together they went for rides into the countryside and practiced their music for camp. Jayden cherished every moment he spent with her.

And every meal time the whole family prayed for his mother.

On Friday morning at the breakfast table, Mr. Morgan announced Mom had been cleared for visitors. He arranged to take the morning off school so he could go with Jayden to see her.

As Mr. Morgan drove to the hospital, Jayden sat quietly looking out the window, nibbling his fingernails. Every now and then, Mr. Morgan stole a glance at him. Jayden knew he should be making conversation, but to be honest, he didn't feel much like talking. Besides, his mind was a-whirl. What would

Mom be like? Would she still look as haggard as she had at the Police Station, or would she be back to normal? What was he going to say to her he hadn't already said? *Had God answered their prayers for her?*

Hunters Hollow Hospital was on the edge of town. Jayden had passed it often, but had never taken much notice of it. After they parked and were walking towards the Mental Health Unit, Mr. Morgan placed his hand on Jayden's shoulder. "Nervous?"

Jayden nodded. From what he'd seen in movies, Mental Hospitals were scary places.

"I can understand that, but don't be too worried, son. They're just people."

Jayden steeled himself as Mr. Morgan held the door open for him. They signed in, walked down a corridor, and found the activities room. Mom was sitting at a table with a group of others playing a game of cards. Still in her pajamas and with a blanket hanging around her shoulders, she was hunched over the cards in her hands.

She glanced up as they approached, her eyes flickering and then lighting up. "Jay!" Tears rolled down her cheeks as she held her hand out to him.

Jayden hesitated. He could still turn around and escape. But how could he do that? He sucked in a breath and stepped closer.

She pulled him to her side, wrapping her arm around his waist. "Everyone, this is my son, Jay." Her voice was thick and didn't quite sound like Mom.

He shuddered and clenched his teeth. *I wish she wouldn't call me Jay.*

The others at the table, a man with long gray hair and eyes that darted from side to side; a girl not much older than Angie, but who clutched her cards so tightly they were bending; and another older woman whose face was vacant, all looked up and stared at him before saying hello.

If only the floor would open up and swallow him, but he had to say something. He glanced at Mr. Morgan for support.

Mr. Morgan stepped closer, placed his hand on Jayden's shoulder, and smiled at the group. "Hello everyone. Good to see you enjoying yourselves."

Jayden's head spun around. *Did Mr. Morgan know these people?*

"Come and join us." The old man with gray hair patted an empty chair.

"Thanks, I might just do that." Mr. Morgan placed his hand on the back of the chair. "Jayden, why don't you go for a walk with your mother?"

Jayden's eyebrows shot up. Mr. Morgan was going to leave him on his own with Mom? What if she did something crazy?

"You'll be all right, son." Mr. Morgan gave him a reassuring nod.

Jayden let out a slow breath. "Okay…"

Mom stood and tucked her hand into the crook of his arm. "Come on, Jay, let's go for a walk."

As Mom led him to the door, Jayden glanced back at Mr. Morgan. He was already engrossed in the game and the others were laughing at something he'd said. Jayden drew his brows together. *How did he do that?*

Mom led him into an enclosed courtyard where they sat on a bench seat. At least it looked nicer out here than inside. A few large potted plants sat in each corner, and the skylights almost made it seem as if they were outside.

Mom pulled a box of cigarettes from the small bag slung over her shoulder, opened the box and slid a cigarette out. Her hands shook as she tried to strike a match.

Jayden was about to tell her she should give them up, but something stopped him. He wasn't here to judge. "Let me help." He took the box from her and struck the match before holding it to the tip of her cigarette.

She held his gaze as she drew long and hard before blowing the smoke out of the corner of her mouth. She drew two more quick puffs before leaning forward and stubbing the cigarette out in the ashtray on the table. She hung her head and began to sob.

Jayden shifted closer and placed his arm around her.

She slowly lifted her head. Tears streamed down her cheeks. "I'm sorry, Jay." Her bottom lip quivered.

A shudder ran through his body. He pulled a tissue from his pocket and handed it to her.

"It… it wasn't meant to be like this." She paused, breathing heavily. "I've made such a mess of everything."

As she sobbed into his chest, Jayden squeezed back his own tears. He hadn't expected her to be like this, but then, maybe he should have. Hadn't they been praying for her?

He inhaled slowly. Her body shook in his arms. He rubbed her back. "It'll be okay, Mom. You'll be all right."

Her sobs eventually eased and she raised her head. "Can you ever forgive me? For everything?"

Everything? Jayden narrowed his eyes and held her gaze. Was she asking him to forgive her for leaving him when he was only a child? Or just for luring him away from Dad under false pretenses? Did she have any idea how her actions had affected him? He drew a deep breath. But how could he not forgive her? God expected it of him, and as hard it would be, and as much as she didn't deserve it, he had no choice. She was broken. She needed help, and at last she seemed to know it.

He released his breath. "Yes, Mom, I forgive you."

She threw her arms around him and began to sob again. He'd never seen her so needy. "Thank you, Jay. You're a good boy. The best."

Moments passed. She straightened and wiped her face.

He changed position and rested his forearms on the table. "So, how are you doing, Mom?"

She blinked. "It's hard to believe Buck's dead."

"You shouldn't have got involved with him."

She hung her head. "I know."

Jayden raised a brow. "I wish you hadn't."

She raised her head. "I should have listened to you."

He nodded.

"He got me hooked on drugs."

"You've got the chance to get clean now. I hope you will."

She pulled the blanket tighter and inhaled deeply.

Jayden studied her. Would she have the strength to stay off them? He prayed she would.

She reached out and squeezed his hand. "I want to, but I don't know if I can."

"The Morgan's will help you. They're great people."

"And what about you, Jay? Will you help me?"

Jayden gulped. "I'm not sure. I might have to go home."

Her brows puckered. "No, don't go, Jay. Please don't leave me."

Here we go again... "I might not have a choice. I'm illegal, you know that."

Her face blanched as she clutched his arm. "Oh, Jay, I need you. Don't worry about that."

He tilted his head as a wave of sadness washed over him. If only he could stay. "I'll be discovered eventually. I'm not sure when I'll be going yet, but it might be sometime soon." He swallowed hard, pushing down the lump growing in his throat. God really had to help him with this.

"It won't be the same without you here, Jay."

"Why don't you come home with me?"

Tears welled in her eyes again. "There's no one there for me."

Jayden pinched his lips. "What about me?" What went on in her brain?

She let out a feeble laugh. "I'm sorry. Of course there's you." She smiled at him as she patted his hand. "I'll think about it."

He gave her the best smile he could manage. "Get better first, okay?"

She nodded. "I need to go back in, Jay. Can you help me?"

He stood and helped her up. As he walked across the courtyard to the door, he stopped, placed his hands on her shoulders and turned her slowly to face him. "I really hope you get better. Try hard?"

Her eyes moistened again as she nodded.

He pulled her close and gave her a big hug. "And Mom, can you please not call me Jay?"

Her head jerked back, her eyes widening. "What do you mean?"

"I hate being called Jay. I much prefer Jayden."

Her hand flew to her cheek. "I had no idea. I'm sorry, Jay." Her shoulders sagged. "I've done it already." She let out a deep sigh.

He leaned forward and placed a kiss on her cheek. "It's okay. Just get yourself better."

Her face softened into a smile, not one of her over-the-top flashy smiles, but one that was genuine, giving him hope that she might just get through this.

MR. MORGAN WAS STILL PLAYING cards when Jayden and Kathryn returned. The other three were genuinely upset when he stood to leave.

"I'll come back as soon as I can."

"Make sure you do." The older woman had a sparkle in her eye.

"You can count on it, Betty." He gave her a friendly smile.

"Bye." She waved as he moved away from the table.

"Mom wants to go back to her room," Jayden said quietly when Mr. Morgan joined them.

"No problem. I'll call a nurse."

Within minutes, Mom was lying in her bed, curled up like a little child, her eyes squeezed shut.

"It's going to be a long road, son." Mr. Morgan placed his hand on Jayden's shoulder as they walked out of the hospital towards the car.

"Yes, but I think she might just make it." Jayden felt a lightness in his chest.

"I think so, too." Mr. Morgan unlocked the car and gave him an encouraging smile before opening the door and climbing inside.

JAYDEN RETURNED to his apartment to pack for camp while Mr. Morgan went back to school. But instead of packing, he flopped onto the sofa and closed his eyes. So much had happened over the last week. In fact, it was like he was caught in a whirlwind and had no idea where he'd land.

After a few moments of rest, he pulled himself up. If he stayed lying down, he'd end up asleep, and then he wouldn't have time to pack before Mr. Morgan came back for him. His guitar caught his attention. He picked it up and began playing some of the songs he and Angie had been practicing. Songs that had now come to mean so much to him. As he played, a sense of God's presence fell on his heart, and a verse that Angie had shared with him came to mind. Jeremiah 29, verse 11, *"For I know the plans I have for you," declares the Lord, "plans to prosper you and not to harm you, plans to give you hope and a future."* While Jayden didn't know what the future held, God did. And that's all that mattered.

CHAPTER 17

*B*en quickly finished packing his small suitcase and zipped it closed.

Tessa sat on the edge of the bed watching his every move. "Are you sure about this?"

"Absolutely. It's time."

"We've been through it countless times, wouldn't it be best to wait for him to decide?"

Ben closed the space between them and placed his hands on her shoulders. "I'm not going to force him, but it'll be easier for him to do the right thing if I'm there to support him."

"Do you want me to come with you?"

He raised a brow. "In your condition?"

She glanced down at her stomach and sighed. "You're right. I doubt the doctor would let me travel anyway."

"For once I want to take the initiative. I feel good about it, but please pray."

She smiled up at him. "Of course. But don't stay away too long."

"I won't, don't worry. I'm not planning on staying any longer than I have to."

"I know, but I'm going to miss you."

Ben stepped closer and gently pulled her towards him. "And I'm going to miss you too." He brushed her cheek with the back of his hand as their eyes met. His heart filled with love for her. He lifted her chin and lowered his lips until they touched. He kissed her slowly, savouring every moment. When he let her go, her face was flushed and her eyes moist.

"Hurry back, Ben." Her voice was soft, barely more than a whisper.

He gave her another slow kiss. "Don't you worry about that. I'll be back as soon as I can."

TESSA CLUNG to Ben and gave him a huge hug before he stepped onto the escalator leading to the departures area of the Brisbane International Airport. Fixing her gaze on him, she waved and blew him one last kiss before he disappeared.

If only she could have gone with him, but having been advised to 'take it easy', they'd agreed that her job was to pray and to look after herself and their unborn baby.

She stepped out of the cool air-conditioned airport into a beautiful late spring day in Brisbane. The sky was a brilliant blue, and as a plane soared upwards, leaving a trail of vapour in its wake, her thoughts drifted. The last couple of months of her pregnancy had been challenging. She'd been so tired all the time, and although she loved her work, especially now she'd returned to her old job as Head Surgeon, she was looking forward to taking a break. But how was she going to cope with Ben being away? They'd hardly spent a night apart since they'd married, except for the couple of days she'd spent at Stephanie's mother's farm before they went to Ecuador.

Tessa came back to the present with a jolt. *Stephanie...* She glanced at her watch and breathed a sigh of relief. Plenty of time. In fact, she'd be early for their lunch date.

When she arrived at the new Waterside Café in New Farm ten minutes early, she chose a table and ordered a coffee, all the while keeping one eye on the car park and one eye on the river. She was just finishing her coffee when Mrs. Trejo's modified van pulled into the car park and stopped under a shady poinciana tree. Mrs. Trejo slid out and waited for Stephanie's wheelchair, with Stephanie in it, to be lowered to the ground. Tessa's heart still ached for her friend every time she thought about her not being able to walk. Mrs. Trejo had been so convinced Stephanie would walk again, but now it seemed highly unlikely. She would be confined to a wheelchair for the rest of her life.

Tessa stood and waved to Mrs. Trejo as she drove off, and waited while Stephanie wheeled herself towards the entrance of the café. At least she had some independence these days, although she still lived on the farm with her mother. Tessa leaned down and hugged her. "Great to see you, Steph."

"And you, Tessa. Hope you're looking after this little one." Her eyes sparkled as she gently ran her hand over Tessa's stomach. "You're getting so big."

Tessa rolled her eyes. "And don't I know it!" She glanced

inside. "I've got a table right on the water. We should be able to get you there without too much problem." She stepped around the wheelchair and placed her hands on the handles.

Stephanie reached out and tapped her hand. "I can do it."

Tessa's hand flew to her chest. "I'm so sorry. I keep forgetting how clever you've become with this thing." She laughed lightly.

"You should see me zip around the farm." Stephanie chuckled as she maneuvered around the tables and chairs to reach the table Tessa indicated. "This is a great spot."

"It is, isn't it? I really love living so close to the river, but sometimes I feel so guilty when I think back to the living conditions in Ecuador. We're very spoiled."

"But you enjoyed your time there." She held Tessa's gaze. "You know, since I've been confined to this chair, I've come to realise it's not so much about your living conditions or what you do, it's what's inside you that counts."

"A very profound statement, Stephanie!"

Stephanie laughed. "I know. I have too much time to think these days!"

Tessa looked up as the waiter came to take their orders. "I'm sorry, we've been so busy chatting we haven't even looked at the menu. What do you suggest?"

The waiter, a young man with dark, curly hair and translucent blue eyes, flashed a smile at them. "Well, for two such beautiful young ladies like yourselves, I'd recommend some share plates. The Lamb Koftas are very good, as is the Baked Camembert served with a baguette and a green tomato chutney."

Tessa glanced at Stephanie and raised a brow.

Stephanie shrugged. "Sounds good to me. We'll have one of each."

"And to drink?" The waiter's pencil was poised above his notepad as he angled his head at Stephanie.

"Sparkling water?" Stephanie glanced at her.

She nodded and smiled. "Thank you." When the waiter left, she sat for a moment, her thoughts turning to Ben. She glanced at her watch. He'd be boarding by now.

"How's Ben feeling about the trip?" Stephanie asked.

Tessa inhaled slowly. It was such a huge thing after such a long and challenging road. Strange to think that Jayden could be home by this time next week if all went well. She let her breath out and lifted her gaze. "Nervous. Excited." Tessa blinked back the tears suddenly pricking her eyes.

"I can understand that. It's hard to believe Jayden's been gone for more than a year."

"Yep, and he's changed so much."

"Do you think he'll come back?"

Tessa shrugged. "I hope so." She glanced at the CityCat pulling away from the terminal on the other side of the river and wiped her eyes. "He seems very attached to his girlfriend, and now this has happened to his mother..."

"Wait, what happened to his mother?"

Tessa drew another breath and proceeded to tell Stephanie all about Buck's murder and Kathryn ending up in a Mental Hospital.

"Wow! And they thought she'd killed him?"

Tessa nodded, looking up as the waiter returned with their share plates. She smiled at him and thanked him before picking up some bread and placing a little cheese on it. "Shouldn't be eating this, but it smells so yummy."

"You'll get fat if you're not careful." Stephanie shot her a playful look, but then laughed as she proceeded to do the same.

Tessa shrugged. "I'm past caring."

"I bet you are. But you're looking great."

"Like a beached whale, you mean?" Tessa looked up and burst out laughing. She took a sip of water and settled herself. "I can't wait to be back to normal." As soon as she said it, she wished she could retract the words. At least she would get back to normal, unlike Stephanie. She touched Stephanie's wrist. "I'm so sorry, Steph. That was thoughtless."

"It's okay. You don't need to tip-toe around me. I can handle things like that."

Tessa shook her head. "I don't know how you're doing it. Sure you're not just putting on a happy face?"

"No, I'm not. God's taught me so much by sticking me in this wheelchair. Sure, I miss not being able to walk, but I kind of knew that from the beginning. It was Mum who found it harder to accept. But it's okay, it really is." She leaned closer. "And I've got something exciting to tell you. The reason we came to the city was for me to meet with the Director of Youth Services. I applied for a job working with disadvantaged kids, and I got it! I'm so excited!"

Tessa threw her arms around Stephanie. Joy for her friend welled within her and bubbled out. "That is the best news." She straightened. "Wait, does that mean you're moving back to the city?"

Stephanie nodded, her eyes shining. "Yes, so I'll be able to help you with this little one when he or she comes."

Tessa let out a happy sigh. "I bet your Mum's not too happy about that."

Stephanie chuckled. "I think she's going to sell the farm."

"No! She can't. I love that place."

Stephanie nodded. "I think she is."

A thought flashed through Tessa's mind. But was she jumping the gun? Maybe she needed to pray about it. But it wouldn't hurt to run the thought past Steph, surely. Hadn't the seed of the idea for Ecuador been planted in her heart just like this one had now been? Maybe that's how God works sometimes, planting spontaneous ideas in people's hearts. Why not? She leaned forward, placing her crossed arms on the table. "Steph, I've got an idea."

Stephanie laughed. "Of course you have. Fire away."

Tessa drew a steadying breath. "I've always loved your mother's farm. In fact, I've often day-dreamed about buying one just like it, but I've never mentioned it to Ben." She paused and drew another breath. "What if Ben and I bought it off your mum, and turned it into a retreat? It could even be used for your disadvantaged youth." Her heart quickened as she uttered the words. It felt so right.

Stephanie's face lit up. "That's a great idea! And Mum would be so happy it was being used to help others."

Tessa straightened. "Ben would have to agree, of course, but I think he would. Since we've been back from Ecuador we've been praying about what we should be doing, and I think this might be the answer. I can see it already… little cabins dotted around where people can stay to unwind and spend quality time with each other and with God. A big communal area for groups, outdoor activities, and animals. Lots of animals!" Tessa couldn't help her enthusiasm. The more she thought about it, the more convinced she became that the idea was from God.

"It sounds great." Stephanie beamed at her. "Now all we need to do is make it happen."

Tessa exhaled slowly. "Yes. We need to pray about it, and then I'll talk to Ben. I'm sure our church would back it too, so we can talk with our Pastor." She leaned forward again and squeezed Stephanie's hand. "I really feel good about this."

"So do I." Stephanie chuckled. "But first you've got to have this baby!"

Tessa laughed. "Yes, that's true." She glanced down and rubbed her tummy. "And it can't happen soon enough!"

The waiter appeared at their table and collected their empty plates. "Can I get you two ladies anything else?"

Tessa looked at Stephanie. "Coffee?"

"That'd be great."

"Two flat whites, thanks."

"Coming right up."

As the waiter weaved his way through the tables, Tessa clutched her stomach and doubled over in pain. She breathed heavily, trying to deal with the sudden excruciating pain stabbing her stomach.

"Tessa, what's happening?" Stephanie wheeled her chair closer to Tessa and draped her arm across her shoulder.

"I think I'm in labour." She clutched her stomach again as another stab of pain hit her.

"You can't be... it's too early."

"I know... and Ben's on his way to America. Oh... I'm going to be sick." Tessa placed her hand over her mouth and tried to hold back the vomit rising in her throat.

The waiter appeared out of nowhere and placed a bowl on her lap. "I'll call an ambulance."

Tessa threw up her whole lunch and more before the ambulance arrived. The paramedics placed her onto a trolley bed and settled her in the ambulance. As they were closing the doors, Stephanie called out that she'd follow as soon as her mother arrived. Tessa could only nod.

CHAPTER 18

*J*ayden sat in the middle row of Mr. Morgan's SUV with his arm around Angie as they sped along the main highway towards Camp Fletcher. His stomach was tight, and despite the coolness in the air, his hands were damp with sweat. In the front, Simon chatted to his father, but he and Angie sat in silence. During the week they'd spent at her place, they'd skirted around the fact that their relationship as they knew it was coming to an end.

He kissed the side of her face, his eyes lingering on the cute ringlets of red hair spiraling down her neck. She turned her head and smiled at him, sending his raw nerves into a whirl. Just as well Mr. Morgan and Simon were in the car, because it was the only thing stopping him from kissing her.

Just as dark settled in, Mr. Morgan turned off the highway and into the entrance to the campsite. Twenty or so cars were already parked in the parking lot, and lights from the main building lit up the surrounding area. A gust of wind barreled into Jayden as he opened the car door. There'd been talk of cancelling the weekend camp because of the threat of bad weather, but the decision had been made to hold it anyway. Maybe not so wise as the wind was already whipping up a storm. He zipped his jacket up and then helped Angie out of the car. The faint tinkling of a piano reached them through the whistling wind.

"We must be late." Jayden had to shout.

"No, they'll just be practicing."

As he grabbed their luggage from the trunk, another car pulled up alongside. Gareth and his girlfriend, Rachel, climbed out.

"Hey Jayden. Good to see you. Ready to jam?" Gareth called out above the wind.

Jayden nodded. "Yep, can't wait."

"Great. Let's get out of this wind."

INSIDE, the main building buzzed with young people chatting and laughing. A casual supper had been prepared for those who hadn't eaten. Jayden carried his guitar to the front of the room where the other instruments were all sitting, and then joined his group of friends around a table. He reached for Angie's hand and held it tightly.

"Sorry to hear about your mother, Jayden." Rachel leaned forward across the table, a concerned look on her face.

Jayden gulped. Word had obviously gotten around. "Thanks." He offered a warm smile.

"Is she going to be okay?"

Jayden let out a breath. "I hope so."

"We're all praying for her."

"Thanks."

"It's the least we can do."

Gareth stood and slapped him on the back. "Come on, time to rock and roll."

Jayden sighed with relief. He couldn't talk like this any longer. He needed to lose himself in some music.

THE BAND BEGAN TO PLAY, and before long all the chairs were filled with young people eager to join in. Jayden glanced at Angie every few seconds, his heart fluttering every time their eyes met. If only there was some way of staying. But he'd looked into it, and there wasn't any option. As soon as the authorities were alerted, he'd have to leave. The good news was that as he was still a minor, he may not be barred from re-entering in the future, but how could he and Angie survive with not seeing each other? His heart ached at the thought.

He glanced up again and studied her as she played. She made it look so easy, and she played so well. There was no doubt in Jayden's mind she'd be selected for a musical scholarship once she graduated from High School. He let out a sigh. The only way it could work would be for him to go home, finish school and then apply for University here as well. But he wanted to study Veterinary Medicine, and it was unlikely he'd get in since places were limited, even if he studied hard. He'd have to study something else, but if it meant being with Angie again, he'd do it. He felt himself growing anxious again, and had to remind himself to trust God, just as the words of the song they were playing said to do.

Pastor Graham walked to the front as the song came to an end. Jayden took a seat with Angie and held her hand. He had no idea how he'd be able to concentrate on the message, but he tried to push all thoughts of leaving aside for the moment to focus his attention on the pastor. There were still a lot of unanswered questions from the study they'd been doing, and he did want to listen.

"Welcome to Camp Fletcher, everyone. We're going to have a great weekend of fun, fellowship and learning, despite the weather." He glanced outside as a gust of wind howled through the trees. "Over the past couple of months, we've been finding out how we can be certain of God's existence. We've studied the creation story, and how recent scientific discoveries are confirming that the universe as we know it was brought into existence by an intelligent being, and instead of refuting the creation story, these discoveries are confirming that it couldn't have just happened by chance, as many scientists and others used to believe. The more they study the complexity of the universe and all the living beings within it, the more proof there is for an intelligent designer. I'm sure you'll all agree it's really exciting stuff. As Christians, we believe that the intelligent designer is God, but how is it possible for us, as mere human beings, to have a personal relationship with a God who's so immense and so powerful? How can God have any relevance in our day to day living? That's the topic of this camp, and I hope that by the end of it, you'll be so in awe of God that you'll never doubt His keen interest and involvement in your life every minute of every day. Let's bow our heads."

Jayden squeezed Angie's hand as he bowed his head. His spirit quickened as Pastor Graham began to pray.

"Lord God, Creator of heaven and earth, and all that is within this great universe, we pause to give You thanks for loving us. You know each one of us by name, You know how many hairs are on our heads, You know our thoughts before we even think them. You know our future, and You know our past. There is nothing You don't know about us. And yet, we often struggle to trust You. We doubt Your love for us. We wonder how You can be involved in our lives when we can't see You. And we wonder if You really care for us when things go wrong, as they so often do. Lord God, please open the eyes of our hearts to You this weekend. Reveal Yourself to us in a special way, and may we all leave this place with the profound assurance that You, the God of all creation, has written your name on our hearts, and that nothing in this world or the next can separate us from Your love, which is perfect and true in every way. Amen."

Jayden brushed his eyes before raising his head. He wasn't the only one who'd been touched—Angie was wiping her eyes too.

As Pastor Graham gave his message, Jayden listened with an eager heart. He'd heard most of it before, but had never really understood it. Tonight, it was a light bulb moment.

"God is God. He's the great 'I am'. He's sovereign. He can choose to do as he wants. Our understanding of who He is so limited. Not until we see Him face to face in eternity will we even have a glimpse of His majesty and power.

"But despite this, God's made it possible for us to know Him personally through a faith relationship with Jesus, His son. Only through Jesus can we be connected to God. Jesus is the door to eternal life, but He's also given us the Holy Spirit to guide and to lead us. Through prayer and Bible study we can come closer to God, but we shouldn't just pray when we need help. We have to develop a relationship with God, much like we develop a relationship with a friend.

"Romans 12:2 says *'Do not be conformed to this world, but be transformed by the renewal of your mind, that by testing you may discern what is the will of God, what is good and acceptable and perfect.'* If we follow what the world says, we'll never grow close to God. The more we study the Bible and pray, the more we'll learn what the will of God is in our everyday lives. Our thoughts will become more in line with God's, and our actions and reactions will reflect His love. God wants us all to have new ways of thinking, new ways of acting. His aim is that we be transformed and freed by the truth of His word. That we allow the fruit of His Spirit—love, joy, peace, patience, kindness, goodness, faithfulness, gentleness and self-control, to grow in our hearts, to love Him with our whole being, and to love our neighbors as we love ourselves. This is the will of God for our lives."

Pastor Graham paused, allowing his gaze to travel around the auditorium. "My challenge to you tonight is this—will you allow God to transform your minds as well as your hearts? I'm not going to drag this out. You'll know if God's working on your heart. If you want to do business with God, come forward as we sing the last song, and tell Him you don't want to be conformed to this world any longer, but that above all, you want to live for Him, and that you'll allow Him to transform you into the young man or woman He wants you to be. One that will show His love to the world; who'll be compassionate and kind. To be God's light in a world filled with darkness. To be God's ambassador here on earth. Come now if you want to do business with God."

Jayden's heart pounded as he stood and walked with Angie to their instruments. He desperately wanted to go forward, but he had to provide the music. As he played, Jayden realised he didn't need to go to the front— he could do business with God right where he was. As he strummed the chords for "Take my Life and Let it Be", he sang the words as well, and gave God every part of his life.

Angie lifted her hand from the keys and wiped her eyes as she played. She was doing business with God as well.

LATER, after the evening program had ended and everyone was having supper, Jayden led Angie to a quiet corner away from the crowd. His pulse quickened at what he was about to do.

CHAPTER 19

essa thought she was going to die. The whole time in the ambulance she threw up, a strange thing to do if she was in labour. It didn't make sense. Plus she had diarrhea as well as stomach cramping. In between vomiting and diarrhea bouts, one of the two paramedics wiped her forehead with a damp cloth, but said very little apart from giving her words of encouragement. As she lay there, gripping her stomach, Tessa occasionally caught the looks that passed between the two paramedics, but couldn't work out what they meant. Were they so worried they couldn't say anything directly to her?

After what seemed an eternity, the ambulance pulled up outside the hospital and within moments she was being wheeled into the Emergency Department. She placed her hands on her stomach and prayed for her unborn baby before she reached for the bowl and vomited up bile. She panted hard. What was happening to her?

A nurse took her vitals and whispered to another nurse. Stephanie and Mrs. Trejo appeared beside her. Stephanie's face was white. A feeling of dread flowed through Tessa's body before another stab of pain hit.

A young female doctor entered the cubicle and placed her hands over Tessa's abdomen. "I'm going to give you an internal, Mrs. Williams."

Tessa's face fell.

"Don't worry, the nurse will clean you up first."

Relief flowed through her. She tried desperately to control her bodily functions whilst being examined. She tried picturing Ben on the plane, and where he'd be right now. Maybe flying over Fiji. She began dry retching. She pushed the vomit back, but her stomach tensed.

"Just relax, Mrs. Williams. Take some deep breaths."

Tessa nodded and tried to breathe deeply, just like she'd been taught at the ante-natal classes she and Ben had been attending. She finally calmed, allowing the doctor to complete the examination.

The doctor stepped back and pulled off her gloves. "Well, I've got some good news for you. You're not in labour." A small grin formed on the doctor's face.

Tessa drew her eyebrows together. "What's wrong with me, then?"

"You've got a bad case of food poisoning."

Tessa struggled to sit. "Food poisoning?"

"Yes. Can you think what you've eaten that might have caused it?"

A nurse arranged some pillows behind her back.

She thought about all the food she'd eaten over the past few days. Lamb Koftas, baked Camembert cheese, *roast chicken from the local store*. That's what it was. She'd had it for lunch yesterday and thought at the time it tasted a little off. *Why did I eat it?* She grabbed her stomach and doubled over as excruciating pain hit her again. She groaned in agony.

The doctor placed her hand on Tessa's back. "We'll do some tests, and keep you in until it passes. We'll need to monitor your baby."

Tessa's head jerked up. "Is something wrong?"

The doctor patted her arm. "No, please don't worry. It's unlikely there's a problem, but best to be sure."

She let out a breath. "Okay." She tried to smile. "Thank you."

"My pleasure. The nurse will look after you. I'll look in on you a little later."

"Thank you."

When the doctor left, Stephanie wheeled herself in and stopped beside Tessa's bed. "Food poisoning, huh?" She angled her head, a grin forming on her face.

"Seems that way." Tessa reached for the bowl again. How much more vomit did she have left? She wiped her mouth and settled her breathing. "I can't take much more of this."

Stephanie squeezed her hand and gave her an encouraging smile. "You'll survive."

Tessa sighed. "I guess so." She straightened. "I need to call Ben."

"No need to worry him. Besides, he wouldn't answer."

"Mmm, you're probably right. I'll send him a text."

"Let me do it? You need to rest." Stephanie picked up the damp face washer and wiped Tessa's brow.

Tessa lowered her head against the pillows. "Thanks. Phone's in my bag." Her eyes flickered and closed.

~

BEN SETTLED into his seat for the long haul flight to Billings, Montana, via Los Angeles and Portland. As the plane banked over Moreton Bay, revealing the sprawling city of Brisbane below, he uttered a quick prayer for Tessa. He hated leaving her, especially in her condition, but there was no way either he or the doctor would have allowed her to travel. She'd told him not to bother calling until he got there, assuring him she'd be fine, but he couldn't help being slightly concerned.

The plane was full, and he was glad he'd chosen an aisle seat. At least he could stretch his legs a little. Once the seat belt light was switched off, he flipped open his laptop and clicked on a client file. Everyone else was busy choosing a movie to watch, but he had work to do, and this was a great opportunity to catch up. But thoughts of Jayden and Tessa kept running through his mind and he finally gave up. There was no way he could concentrate.

Maybe he should have forewarned Jayden instead of turning up unannounced. What if Jayden didn't want to see him? But Robert Morgan had convinced him it was the right thing to do. Ben ran his hand slowly over his head, lowered the seat back, and tried closing his eyes, but he couldn't get comfortable. A baby a few seats further back began crying. He sat up and flicked through the movies until he found one he might like.

The flight seemed never-ending, and this was only the first

leg. He had a long lay over in L.A., but all going well, he should arrive at Billings by six p.m. Robert said it'd take two hours to drive to the camp from there.

When Ben finally arrived at L.A International Airport early Friday morning local time, he immediately switched his phone on. The message from Stephanie alarmed him. *'Tessa's in hospital, but don't worry—it's only food poisoning. The baby's fine.'* But *hospital?* Why would Tess be in hospital if it was only food poisoning? And what had she eaten? He calculated what time it was back home. It was the wee hours of the morning there. Should he call? He sighed. There was nothing he could do, anyway. Maybe he should wait until he reached Portland, although he could call the hospital. But Steph hadn't said which hospital. Best to wait. But it was so long until he'd arrive in Billings.

His phone dinged. He looked down. A message from Robert. His heart fell. Not more bad news, surely? He clicked on the message and opened it. His shoulders sagged. *'Bad weather here, your flight might be delayed. Sorry. Will be in touch, Robert'.* As if the flight wasn't long enough already. He went to the Information Counter. Robert was right. All flights to Billings were currently being diverted due to bad weather. He'd need to wait in Portland until it cleared.

No use getting upset. Nothing could be done about the weather, but he felt restless during the four-hour layover. He just wanted to get there and see Jayden. And he needed to find out what had happened to Tess. He found a seat and tried to read, and even opened his laptop again, but he still couldn't focus. Strange how alone he felt in such a busy airport. But he wasn't alone. God was with him, and he needed to trust that all would work out. He rested his head in his hands and prayed.

When Ben raised his head, an older man with scruffy clothes had taken a seat opposite him. Ben's heart quickened. Had God placed this man here for him to talk to? He smiled at the man and began chatting. The man's face brightened. He told Ben he was on his way to see his daughter who'd just been diagnosed with cancer. Ben's heart went out to the man, and he spent the next hour talking with him. Before the man left, Ben prayed with him—something he would never have done before Ecuador.

Ben called Tessa as soon as he disembarked at Portland. Although he had peace in his heart that she was okay, he couldn't help the small amount of anxiety he felt as he waited for her to answer. When he heard her voice, he swallowed hard. "Tess, what happened?"

"Oh Ben, I thought I was going to die. But I'm okay now. I'll be going home shortly." Her voice sounded weak.

"You had me worried."

"I'm sorry. I thought I was in labour to start with, so at least it wasn't that." She let out a small chuckle.

"Well that's a relief. Is Stephanie with you?"

"No, she had to go, but Mum and Dad are coming for me."

"I'm glad about that. So are you really okay?"

"Yes Ben, I'm really okay. And so's the baby."

He let out a relieved sigh. "Thank God for that."

They continued chatting for a while. He told her about the expected delay, but that he'd determined not to let it frustrate him. She told him she was praying for his meeting with Jayden.

He thanked her and told her he loved her. She told him she missed him already and to call again soon.

When he hung up, he checked the Departures Board which confirmed that his connecting flight to Billings had been indefinitely delayed due to bad weather.

He lined up at the Information Counter and inquired about the possibility of hiring a car. The airline attendant advised against it. "It's pretty hairy out there, sir. Best to wait for the weather to clear."

He let out a small sigh, and then chastised himself. Hadn't he determined not to get frustrated? He took the attendant's advice and accepted a hotel room for the night. Although he would have liked to have seen Jayden tonight, a good night's sleep in a proper bed would do him good.

He pressed the button for the elevator and got out at the fifth floor. When he opened the door to the room, he placed his suitcase on the rack, pulled out his washbag and a change of clothes, and jumped into the shower.

As the warm water ran down his body, he closed his eyes. Never had a shower felt so good.

CHAPTER 20

*J*ayden wrapped his hands around his mug of hot chocolate. His heart pounded as he gazed at his gorgeous Angie.

She took a sip of her drink and then placed her mug on the table. "What do you want to talk about, Jayden?"

She looked so sweet, and his heart ached with love for her. He had to trust that somehow it would all work out. Lowering his mug to the table he shifted closer and took her hand. He cleared his throat. "Angie, this is the hardest thing I've ever done, but tonight I had a real sense that I need to go home."

Her eyes widened.

"God didn't tell me directly, but I had the strongest feeling that it was the right thing to do, and I can't ignore it any longer." He brushed tears from his eyes.

Angie blinked as her eyes misted over as well. "I knew it would happen one day soon, and as much as I don't want you to go," her voice caught, "I agree with you—it's the right thing to do."

Tears stung his eyes as his chest burned with anguish. "I love you, Angie." His chest heaved.

"And I love you too, Jayden." Tears streamed down her face.

Their eyes were locked.

"When will you go?"

He inhaled slowly. "After camp. Early next week." Was he really saying this? He'd be going home so soon?

She nodded. "God will honor your decision. He's got good things planned for you."

It was Jayden's turn to nod. He didn't trust his voice.

"We should pray." Angie wiped her face.

Jayden sniffed. "We should." He took her hand and squeezed it before closing his eyes. "Lord God, thank You for bringing Angie into my life. You know how much I love her, and how much it's hurting me to let her go, but I pray that You'll bless her and that You'll use her in whatever way you see fit in the future. She's such a special person, Lord, and she loves You so much. Please help us both to grow in You, and to always put You first in everything we do. In Jesus' name, Amen."

Angie leaned closer. "And Lord God, please bless Jayden's obedience. Go with him as he returns to his family, heal their hurting hearts, and bring them closer to each other and to You. And Lord, I pray for Jayden's mom. Please work in her life and soften her heart. May she come to know Your love in a real way. Thank You for the time Jayden and I had together." She paused and inhaled deeply. "You know how special he is to me, and he always will be. Look after him, Lord. Pour your blessings out on him, and wrap Your arms around him. Give him strength and wisdom as he goes home. In Jesus' precious name, Amen."

He pulled her close and cuddled her. He kissed the top of her head and squeezed back tears. How could doing the right thing hurt so much?

Moments passed. He wished time would stand still. Angie finally raised her head and looked at him. "Can you hear that?"

He angled his head. "Hear what?"

She chuckled. "Nothing."

He drew his eyebrows together. What was she talking about?

"The wind's stopped."

She was right. The only noise came from the chatter and laughter of campers. The howling had stopped. "Shall we take a walk?"

She smiled up at him. "That would be nice."

He held her hand as they ventured outside.

With the wind stopped, an eerie hush had settled. Fresh pine needles crunched under foot as he led her along the formed path toward the lookout. Not that there'd be much to see. Clouds still hovered overhead, and the only light came from his cell phone which he used to light their way. They passed one or two others on their way back, and another couple was ahead of them. He wrapped his arm around her shoulders as they walked in silence.

They reached the lookout and stood against the metal railing. It was difficult to see where the mountains met the sky, but Angie assured him they were out there. A light mist was forming, and he pulled her closer. "Are you warm enough, Ange?"

She nodded, but snuggled into his chest anyway.

Although he'd done the right thing, his heart was heavy. How long would it be until he'd see her again?

He nuzzled the top of her head. The smell of her freshly washed hair made him weak. If only he could kiss her.

She lifted her head.

He bit his lip. His eyes caressed her face as he drank in everything about her. He gazed into her eyes. "Can I kiss you, Angie?" His voice was weak, breathless.

She didn't answer, but instead lifted her mouth to his.

Jayden kissed her slowly and gently, savoring every second. This kiss had to sustain them both for a long time. When he eventually pulled away, her eyes glistened. His arms tightened around her as he committed this moment to memory.

BEN HAD SET his alarm for five a.m. If the weather had improved, the first flight to Billings would be scheduled for seven a.m. He raised the blind and looked outside. The wet road glistened under the streetlights as early morning traffic trundled along, but at least it was only a drizzle. He flipped his phone open and checked his emails. Yes, one from the airline. He clicked on it. His flight had been rescheduled and was due to leave at seven. He let out a relieved sigh and quickly dressed and packed the few things he'd taken out.

Arriving at the airport in plenty of time, he chose a small café near his departure lounge and ordered a light breakfast.

He selected a financial newspaper off the rack and flicked through it while he waited for his meal to be delivered, but pushed it aside when he couldn't recall a thing he'd read. How could he concentrate when he'd be seeing Jayden in a matter of hours?

He toyed with his food, but downed a full cup of coffee and ordered another. When his flight was called, he jumped up and strode to the boarding gate.

Three hours later, Ben's plane began the descent into Billings Logan International Airport. The sight of huge mountain ranges, icy blue lakes and rivers spreading out in every direction as far as the eye could see took his breath away.

But then his shoulders sagged. Had Jayden seen a bear up close? Had he been to Yellowstone National Park? Had he been horse riding? He would have experienced so many things he and Tessa hadn't been part of. After living out here, how would Jayden ever adjust to living back in the city? Ben inhaled slowly. *Lord, I trust You to prepare the way. Please don't let me make a mess of it.*

HEADING NORTH ALONG HIGHWAY 87, Ben's hands gripped the steering wheel. He barely noticed the magnificent countryside —his entire focus was on Jayden.

CHAPTER 21

The following morning, Jayden woke to the sound of worship music playing through the speakers in the cabin he shared with five other boys. Much better than his normal alarm, but it was still way too early. Turning over, he buried his head in his pillow and began drifting back to sleep. Images of Angie floated through his mind, and warmth flowed through his body. All of a sudden his head jerked up. He'd told Angie he was going home. The warmth drained out of his body and in its place, a deep pain gripped his heart. His head flopped back onto his pillow as a guttural groan slid from his throat.

Had he really told Angie he was leaving, or was it just a bad dream? His heart burned. *Oh God, what have I done?*

The music grew louder. He covered his ears with his pillow, but the words filtered through.

Change my heart oh God
Make it ever true
Change my heart oh God

May I be like You.

He squeezed back the tears pricking his eyes. It was real. He'd told her, but he'd also given God his life to do with as He pleased. He'd asked God to mold him and make him, like clay in the potter's hands. Tears flowed as the rest of the song played, and God's Spirit reached deep into his heart.

Rolling over, Jayden drew his knees to his chin and wrapped his arms around them. His head hung heavily on his arms as tears rolled down his cheeks. His chest heaved. *Oh Lord, please change my heart. Help me to think and feel like You do. Please mold me and shape me into the person You want me to be. I'm sorry for being so stubborn and selfish. I know going home is the right thing to do, but it's so hard letting go of Angie, dear Lord.* He sniffed and wiped his face with the back of his hand. *Please help me to let her go, for now at least.* He let out a long, slow breath and remained still and silent as he allowed the praise and worship music to touch his soul.

A soft knock, followed by the voice of one of the leaders, stirred Jayden out of his prayerful state.

Below him on the bottom bunk, bed springs squeaked as Gareth moved.

Matt called out from the top of another bunk and said they'd heard, before burying his head in his pillow.

Jayden inched his way to the ladder at the end of the bed and climbed down backwards. The others began to stir and one by one sat and stretched before climbing out of bed and preparing for the day.

Angie was already seated in the dining room when he and the boys entered a short while later. She waved for them to join her and her group of friends. He steeled himself before walking over and taking a seat beside her. Memories of their kiss quickened his pulse, but then he stared at his hands. He needed to control his thoughts. If his commitment to God was sincere and genuine, he needed to be more careful with what he allowed to flow through his mind. Not that kissing Angie was wrong, but if it dominated his thinking, then it was. Today he would try to enjoy her company as a friend, and not so much as his girl-friend, as hard as that might be.

He gave her the best smile he could muster and began breakfast.

THE MORNING'S program included a time of praise and worship followed by small group discussions. Jayden put his all into both as he sought God's strength to follow through with his decisions. During the free time just prior to lunch, he joined a game of volleyball in the gymnasium, and as much as he tried to keep his eyes off Angie, the flash of her red hair caught his eye every time she made a move. He'd just punched the ball over the net when a car pulling up outside the main entrance caught his attention through the window. Not the car so much as the person getting out of it. His eyes popped. It sure looked like Dad. But it couldn't be—what would Dad be doing here? The ball came back over the net. It should have been an easy hit as it headed straight for him, but his attention was elsewhere. The ball bounced on the ground beside him.

"Jayden! How'd you miss that?" Gareth shot him a puzzled look and then picked the ball up and punched it to the server on the other team.

Jayden stepped out of the marked play area and walked to the window.

Angie joined him, placing her arm around his shoulder. "What's wrong, Jayden?" Her voice was soft and full of concern.

His gaze didn't shift. Mr. Morgan stepped outside and shook the man's hand before pointing towards the gymnasium. As the man turned, Jayden gasped.

Angie followed Jayden's gaze. "Who's that with Dad?"

Jayden's lip quivered. This couldn't be happening. But it was. "It's my dad." His voice was barely a whisper.

"Your dad?" Angie's arm stiffened on his shoulder as she turned to face him. "Jayden, is that really your dad?" Her gaze flickered back to the two men approaching.

He nodded slowly before he walked to the entrance of the building.

Dad stopped a few feet outside. His eyes had tears in them.

Jayden's heart pounded as tears stung his own eyes. "Dad..." He could hardly speak.

Dad stepped forward and drew Jayden into his arms. "Jayden..."

"I'm sorry, Dad."

"It's all right, son."

Jayden closed his eyes and for the first time in his life, hugged his dad with everything he had.

LATER, Jayden introduced Dad to Angie. He pulled her to his side and slipped his arm around her waist. He'd never expected this moment to happen. His chest filled with pride. "Dad, this is Angie."

A warm smile grew on Dad's face as he leaned forward and kissed her cheek. "Nice to meet you, Angie."

"And you, Mr. Williams." Angie's voice was so sweet.

Mr. Morgan cleared his throat. "Angela, we should give them some time. Come with me?"

She nodded and then gave Jayden a hug. "I'll see you soon."

He drew a breath, his gaze lingering on her for a moment before she moved away with her father.

JAYDEN TURNED and faced his father. So unexpected to be standing here with him, but so good.

"Let's take a walk," his dad said.

Jayden nodded.

Dad placed his arm on Jayden's shoulder as they strolled to the lake. They sat on the ground and gazed at the snow-capped mountains in the distance. A gentle breeze blew across the lake which was shimmering under the wide open sky. Brightly colored fall leaves ruffled lightly in the breeze. Some fluttered slowly to the ground, adding to the multi-colored carpet covering the area.

Over the next hour, Jayden poured his heart out to his father. He shared how hurt and disappointed he'd been when he realized he'd been tricked by his mother, but how he gradually accepted that he couldn't leave her. She needed him, more than he needed her. He struggled to contain his raw emotion as he recalled to Dad about the early days back in Miami, where he lived in the lap of luxury, and then in Austin, Texas, where he almost got tangled up with drugs, partying and girls, and about the road trip north in Mom's old car, and finally ending up in Hunters Hollow, where he met Angie, and the Lord.

"Some kind of year you've had," Dad said, his voice thick with emotion.

Jayden lifted his gaze and met Dad's. Tears brimmed in his eyes and his chest burned. "I have." He swallowed hard.

"Tessa and I never stopped praying for you."

"I know. Thank you." Jayden sniffed and swallowed again before exhaling slowly. "I've decided to come home." Tears streamed down his cheeks.

Dad's eyes widened before he threw his arms around Jayden. "That's the best news you could have given me."

Jayden clung to him. "I only decided last night." He struggled to speak. "I told Angie…" He pushed down the sobs rising in his throat. He straightened, and tried to control his breathing. "I told her it was time for me to go home, that it was the right thing to do. Last night when Pastor Graham was speaking, I got this sense that I needed to let her go, and that God wanted me back home with you and Tessa."

"You don't know how much that means to me. When I decided to come, I had no idea what the outcome would be, but I didn't expect you to have already decided. That is such a bonus. I didn't want to have to convince you. It's so much better that you've already decided. But what about your mother? What's going to happen with her?"

"The Morgan's have said they'll look after her. They're such kind people. They're amazing, in fact. You should stay for a few days and get to know them."

"I'd like that." Dad gave him a warm smile.

"But now we should have lunch. I'm starving."

"That hasn't changed." Dad let out a small chuckle.

"No, that hasn't changed."

BEN WALKED BACK to the main building with Jayden. He wasn't that hungry, but Jayden obviously was. He couldn't get over how much Jayden had grown in just over a year. When he'd left he was just a boy; now he was a young man. And what a young man he'd become. Ben's heart swelled with pride as he glanced at his son.

Lunch was finished, but the cook had kept meals aside for them. They took their plates and sat at a table.

"When were you thinking of coming home?"

Jayden finished his mouthful and lifted his gaze. "Sometime next week."

Ben's eyes widened. "So soon?"

Jayden nodded. "I might change my mind if I wait."

"Angie seems nice."

The corners of Jayden's mouth lifted. "She's the best."

Ben leaned back in his chair and tried to hide the grin forming on his face. His son was in love! How could that have happened? He was so young, but he'd been through so much, and Angie had been there for him when he needed someone to love him. Ben should be grateful it had been her, someone who loved the Lord deeply and who really cared for him, and not that girl from Austin. God had truly been looking after him.

He sat forward and rested his arms on the table. "You're

doing a very mature thing. You're only young, and you don't know what's ahead of you, but you and Angie can always remain as friends."

Jayden winced. It obviously wasn't what he wanted, which was perfectly understandable, but they'd both survive. Life would go on, and in time they'd meet other people.

The door swung open and Robert and Angie walked towards them. Robert had his arm around her shoulders. Angie's eyes were red and she dabbed a tissue to her nose as they reached the table.

Robert raised his eyebrows. "All okay?"

Ben glanced at Jayden and his heart warmed. Yes, everything was okay. In fact, it was more than okay—it was wonderful. He rubbed Jayden's back and nodded.

BEN STAYED for the remainder of camp and spent time with Jayden, Angie and Mr. Morgan. He sat towards the back with Mr. Morgan during the praise and worship sessions, a broad smile planted on his face. Occasionally Jayden lifted his head and met his gaze. Each time, he couldn't stop the grin that spread warmth through his body. Dad was proud of him, and that made the world of difference. No longer did he fear being a disappointment. Dad loved him unconditionally, just like God did. If only he'd realised that a year ago. But if he had, his and Angie's paths might never have crossed, and he would have missed meeting the most beautiful girl in the world. Even if she could now only be his friend.

CHAPTER 22

The next few days passed all too quickly. Dad helped Jayden pack up his apartment, went with him when he said good-bye to Charmian and her family, and sat outside while he and Mr. Morgan visited Mom again.

"Are you sure you won't come in?" Jayden asked as he closed the car door.

Dad shook his head. "No, you go. Just tell her I forgive her."

Jayden's shoulders sagged. Maybe it was for the best. Mom might not cope with seeing Dad after all this time, and she still wasn't well. "Okay, we won't be long."

"Take as long as you need."

Jayden gave him a grateful smile. Dad had changed. He seemed more patient, more caring, more understanding. Jayden still had trouble picturing him building a school playground in Ecuador, but it had obviously done him good. He lifted his hand in a wave and followed Mr. Morgan inside.

Jayden steeled himself as Mr. Morgan signed them in. Mom

wasn't going to be happy about him leaving. He really hoped she wouldn't cause a scene.

The main area where she'd been last time they'd visited was empty. Magazines, empty coffee mugs, and half-finished board games sat on the tables. The nurse told them Mom was in a relaxation class, but it should be finished any minute. Mr. Morgan suggested they wait in the courtyard.

Since Dad had arrived, Jayden hadn't talked to Mr. Morgan on his own. Sitting opposite him now, Jayden felt a tinge of sadness sweep though him. He'd developed a high regard for this man, and he'd miss him when he and Dad flew out tomorrow.

"I'm glad it all worked out, son."

Jayden let out a slow breath. "Yes. But there's still the little problem of me getting through Security."

"You'll be fine. At least you have your dad with you."

Jayden nodded. How scary it would have been if he'd had to go through on his own.

"Do you forgive me for calling your dad?"

Jayden laughed. "What do you think?"

"I think that's a yes." Mr. Morgan let out a chuckle as a door opened and a group of patients walked along the corridor.

Jayden turned his attention to the group. Would Mom remember to call him by his full name? But it didn't really matter. He felt bad he'd made a fuss about it now.

She was at the back of the group, busy talking with Betty and didn't notice him and Mr. Morgan as she walked past. Mr. Morgan stood and caught up with her, tapping her lightly on the back.

She stopped and turned. Her face brightened. "Jayden!

You've come back!" Her over-the-top-smile had returned, and Jayden laughed. She flew into the courtyard and wrapped her arms around him, almost knocking him over.

"Good to see you, Mom." He beamed a smile at her. It really was good to see her back to normal. And she'd remembered his name!

"Sit and talk with me." She pulled him to a bench seat and sat with her legs crossed, leaning forward. Her eyes had cleared and some color had returned to her face. Even her hair had been brushed and washed and had a shine to it. She peered into his eyes. "They're letting me out soon. I can come live with you then."

Jayden gulped. He'd been dreading breaking the news to her. "Remember last time I said I might be going home because I'm illegal?"

Her body stiffened.

"I'm leaving tomorrow, Mom."

She grabbed his hand. "No, Jay, you can't. Please don't go."

"I have to. I'm sorry."

Mr. Morgan stepped forward. "We'll look after you, Kathryn. There's a lovely place not far out of town where you can stay until you're fully well. And Beth and I will be here for you."

Her eyes filled with tears. "I don't know why you'd bother, but thank you." Her gaze shifted back to Jayden. "But Jay, are you sure you can't stay?"

Jayden squeezed her hand. "Yes, Mom, I have to go. But come home when you're better. I'll be there for you."

"Your dad won't like that."

"Dad's okay. He said to tell you he's forgiven you."

A wistful expression grew on her face. "He's a good man, your dad." Tears spilled from her eyes. "I treated you both badly."

"It's okay, Mom." Jayden swallowed hard. "We've both forgiven you."

"Why would you do that? I don't deserve it."

"Because that's what God expects of us."

She sniffed and brushed her face with her hand. Her eyes flickered before she lifted her gaze. "Do you think He'd ever forgive me?"

He smiled at her, pushing back tears of his own. "Of course He will. You just have to ask Him."

She inhaled slowly. "I'll give it some thought."

"You do that. I'll be praying for you every day." Leaning forward, he wrapped his arms around her. "I love you, Mom."

"I love you too, Jayden. Look after yourself." She wiped her eyes.

He sniffed. "I will. Good-bye, Mom." He kissed her cheek and stood. He had to leave so she wouldn't see the tears streaming down his face.

"THAT WAS a hard thing to do, son." Mr. Morgan placed his hand lightly on Jayden's shoulder.

Jayden nodded, not trusting himself to speak.

"She's still got a long way to go, but the Rehab center is great, and I have every hope she'll make a full recovery."

Jayden nodded again, shivering as he stepped outside.

Dad crossed the road and joined them. "How did it go?"

"She was upset, but we think she'll be okay."

Dad smiled. "I hope so."

From there, Mr. Morgan drove to school and collected Angie and Simon. Jessica had stopped going, but was studying online at home so she could finish her schooling.

Angie sat in the back with Jayden and Simon. Jayden took her hand and held it tightly. They had less than twenty-four hours left as boyfriend and girlfriend. His heart quickened as she rested her head on his shoulder.

The Morgan's had invited all of their friends over for a farewell dinner, and even though he'd miss them, Jayden would rather have spent his last night with just the family, but he hadn't had enough courage to tell them that. They were so kind and thoughtful, and he was going to miss them so much.

When they arrived home, the smell of freshly baked bread and roast turkey greeted them. He was sure going to miss Mrs. Morgan's baking. But Tessa's mum's cooking was pretty good, and maybe Tessa's cooking had improved. Over the past few days his thoughts had been turning more towards home. Sometimes they filled him with anticipation, like when images of Bindy and Sparky came to mind, but other thoughts filled him with dread, like going back to school. It was a means to an end, but how could he ever settle into the same old boring routine again? Especially if Neil had made new friends. And besides, Neil would be a year ahead now. He sighed. *Lord, You're going to have to help me with this.*

Mrs. Morgan and Jessica were busy in the kitchen with food preparation. Mrs. Morgan raised her head from her chopping board and smiled. "Help yourselves. There's fresh cookies in the jar, and a ton of pancakes."

Simon raced straight for the pancakes. "Thanks, Mom."

Angie stepped close to her mom and kissed her cheek. "What can I help with?"

Mrs. Morgan patted her hand. "Nothing. You don't want to spend your last afternoon with Jayden in the kitchen. Go for a walk or a ride." Her eyes held a sparkle. What a special woman.

Angie gave her a hug. "As long as you're sure."

Mrs. Morgan waved her hand. "Yes, I'm sure."

Angie didn't notice the look on Jessica's face. Jayden's heart went out to Jess. Not only was she pregnant, but her boyfriend had deserted her. But she couldn't have asked for better parents. It was going to be hard on her, but he was confident she'd be okay.

"What would you like to do? Walk or ride?" Angie smiled at him.

She had to ask? He laughed. "Ride, of course." He turned to Dad and raised a brow. "Like to come?"

Dad chuckled. "No, you two go. You don't want me with you."

"Thanks." Jayden gave him a grateful smile.

"Be back by five," Mr. Morgan called out as they headed towards the door.

"Five. Sure thing," Angie called back.

Jayden checked his watch. An hour. Not long, but long enough.

Angie grabbed his hand and together they ran to the stables. They quickly saddled and mounted the horses, and within minutes they were galloping towards the mountains.

Jayden breathed in the clean, crisp air, his eyes taking in the magnificent surroundings for the last time.

Angie slowed her horse to a trot, as did he. They rode

alongside each other for the next ten minutes until they reached the edge of a ridge where they dismounted and tethered the horses to a tree.

Jayden wrapped his arms around Angie's waist from behind and rested his head on her shoulder. He drank in not only the vista but the whole experience, etching it into his memory. God's creation—the snow-capped mountains, the vast sky, the deep valley below, the stars he couldn't see but were up there, stretching further than he could ever imagine, the birds soaring above, the smell of fresh pine needles, the sound of wind whispering through the trees. His spirit quickened as the verses from Colossians 1 that Pastor Graham often referred to came to mind: *'For by Him all things were created, in heaven and on earth, visible and invisible, whether thrones or dominions or rulers or authorities—all things were created through Him and for Him. And He is before all things, and in Him all things hold together.'* Jayden thought his heart would burst. The God of creation was here with them now, showering His love down on them, filling them with peace and hope for the future.

No words were needed. Jayden pulled Angie tighter and gave thanks to God for bringing her into his life, and asked Him for strength to let her go.

The ride back was slower than the ride out, but they made it back right on the dot of five. The next few hours passed in a blur. Their friends arrived. They laughed, they played games, the boys had a game of pool. Dad talked at length with Mr. and Mrs. Morgan. Jayden wondered what they were talking about. Maybe he'd ask him tomorrow on the plane. Mr. Morgan lit a fire, and towards the end of the evening, they all sat around it and played guitars and sang praise and worship songs in between toasting marshmallows and drinking hot chocolate.

Jayden's heart was full to brimming as he lay on his back with Angie beside him and gazed up at the stars. He turned to her and nuzzled her neck. "We could stay here all night. What do you think?"

She giggled. "We'd freeze, and besides, Dad wouldn't let me."

She was right, it was a silly idea. But maybe they could stay up and watch movies inside. He'd have plenty of time to sleep on the plane, and Angie was taking the day off school.

Her parents agreed, but only if Simon stayed with them. Simon, their chaperone. Understandable, given Jessica's situation.

Angie chose the first two movies—Jayden groaned at her choices but watched them anyway. He chose the next two, and then it was her turn to groan.

As the first pale light of dawn broke on the horizon, Jayden yawned and turned the television off. Time to shower and do a final pack.

CHAPTER 23

The next morning, Jayden and Angie were the first ones ready. They set the table for breakfast as everyone else showered and dressed. By six a.m., everyone was seated around the large kitchen table giving thanks and praying for the days and weeks ahead.

By six-thirty they were headed for Billings International Airport, a two-hour drive away. Angie joined Jayden in Dad's car, but sat in the back while Jayden sat in the front, and Simon went with his parents. Jessica stayed home.

Jayden tried to talk, and kept turning around to look at Angie, but with Dad seated beside him, it was awkward. Angie didn't seem to mind, or maybe chatting the whole way was her method of coping. She pointed out places of interest to Dad, and laughed at his jokes that weren't funny. And all the time, Jayden struggled to ignore the heavy weight lodged in his stomach.

. . .

B<small>EFORE HE WAS READY</small>, they arrived at the airport. As he climbed out of the car, his heart beat in his throat. This was it. He was going home. Dad opened the trunk and lifted out their luggage. Jayden had given his black and green duffle bag to Simon, replacing it with the largest suitcase available to fit in all the things he'd collected during his time in America. He pulled the handle out and placed his carry-on bag and guitar on top of the case, then took Angie's hand and walked into the terminal.

His hands grew clammy as he and Dad joined the line to check in. Dad had told him it would be fine, he wouldn't be stopped, but what if he got pulled aside and questioned about why he'd overstayed? Dad told him not to worry—he was a minor, and he was leaving the country with his father. It wouldn't be a problem. But still, as they approached the counter, his hands shook and his heart pounded.

The tall, attractive woman behind the counter waved them over. Dad handed her their tickets and passports.

Jayden held his breath as she opened both passports and placed them on the counter. "Enjoy your stay, Mr. Williams?" Her eyes darted between her monitor, Dad and the passports while she typed.

Dad cleared his throat. "Yes, thanks. Not long enough, though."

Jayden's shoulders slumped. Why did Dad say that? *Now she'll wonder why I stayed so long.*

She finished with Dad's passport and then placed Jayden's on top. She studied his passport photo, then her gaze shifted to him.

Jayden's body tensed. *God, please let it be okay.* He had long hair in the photo and was just a kid. He looked totally different now.

"Grown up a bit, I see." Her large blue eyes twinkled as a playful grin appeared on her face. As she typed, her attention turned to the screen. Her brows lifted. She leaned closer to the screen, then glanced back at Jayden.

His heart was beating so loudly he was sure she'd hear it.

Dad placed his hand on Jayden's shoulder as he spoke to the woman. "Everything all right?"

How did Dad sound so calm? Jayden's body relaxed. He didn't need to worry, Dad was with him, clean-looking and smart, and his deep voice held authority.

The woman looked up and smiled as she returned the passports. "Yes, everything's fine. Here are your boarding passes. Safe trip."

Dad gave her a warm smile as he tucked the passports and passes into his top pocket. "Thank you."

As Jayden turned and walked towards Angie, he wore a wide grin on his face, and his heart was no longer weighed down.

"Everything okay?" Angie asked when he rejoined the group.

He nodded. "Yep, touch and go for a while, but it's all good. She didn't even ask." He glanced at Dad chatting with Mr. And Mrs. Morgan. "Helped having Dad there."

"Your dad's a good man, Jayden."

Jayden swallowed hard. "I know." He took a deep breath. "He's the best."

The adults shifted closer. "There's time for a quick coffee," Mr. Morgan said. "My treat."

They all moved to an airport café and sat at a table over-looking the runway. Mr. Morgan placed the orders and then everyone chatted while they waited.

Jayden squeezed Angie's hand.

She turned to him and gave him the sweetest smile. Her eyes glistened. The countdown was on and they both knew it. They drank their sodas and nibbled their muffins, but it was like they were on conveyor belts that would soon separate and take them in opposite directions.

"I'm going to miss you, Jayden." Tears welled in the corners of her eyes.

"I'm going to miss you, too, Angie." He blinked back tears of his own.

"I'll write."

"I'll call."

Angie giggled. "We can Facetime."

Jayden nodded. But it wouldn't be the same. They couldn't hold hands; he'd miss the smell of her freshly washed hair and her perfume; they couldn't ride into the mountains, and they wouldn't be able to play music together. He swallowed hard. Yes, he was going to miss her.

"Come on, you two love birds," Mr. Morgan's voice held a tinge of amusement. "Let's have a quick prayer and then it's time."

Jayden gave Angie's hand a squeeze before they shifted their chairs closer.

Mr. Morgan's gaze traveled around the group before it settled on Jayden.

Jayden fidgeted with his hands. He didn't want to be the center of attention.

"Jayden, we've only known you for a short time, but we've all come to love you, and we pray that as you go home to your family, you'll remember your time here with us fondly, as you no doubt will," he grinned at Angie, "but please know you'll always be welcome here." He gave him a warm smile. "Let's pray." Mr. Morgan stood and moved behind Jayden, placing his hand on Jayden's shoulder. Mrs. Morgan stretched out her hand too. "Dear God, we commit Jayden to You today. We ask You to go with him, and that You'll help him grow closer to You. Please help him adjust to life back home, and bless his obedience, dear Lord. May he become a man of God, full of your love and compassion. Guide him and lead him, dear Lord, we pray. Amen."

Jayden wiped his face and sniffed. He would remember this time as long as he lived.

Tears streamed down Angie's face when Jayden gave her one last hug in front of the Security barrier. "I love you, Ange, I always will." He kissed her forehead and brushed her tears with his hand.

"I love you, too, Jayden." She could barely speak.

He squeezed her hand and then gazed into her eyes one last time before turning and entering the security area. His heart was heavy. How would he survive?

He turned and waved after passing through. Mrs. Morgan held Angie tight in her arms.

Angie lifted her hand and waved. Although her face was pale and blotched from crying, she was still the most beautiful girl in the world.

. . .

THEY PASSED through Security without a problem. The flight home was long and tiring—two long transits and a long-haul flight. Jayden filled his time with sleeping, watching movies, eating and some reading. But it was hard to concentrate on anything. He'd left Angie behind, and his thoughts turned to what life would be like at home.

TESSA BUSIED herself preparing for Jayden and Ben's return. She and Ben had discussed how challenging the first few days might be for Jayden, and had decided a few days away at the beach would help him adjust. They'd booked a house at Noosa Heads on the Sunshine Coast for five days, and she was looking forward to leisurely walks on the beach, dining out at one of the many restaurants in the area, and just relaxing prior to the birth of their baby. Jayden would need more activity than that, but Ben could sort that.

Tessa's parents were eager to be at the airport with her, and arranged to meet her there at six-thirty a.m. on the Thursday morning. They arrived only a few minutes apart, and walked into the Arrivals area together.

Her father found three seats, and for the next thirty minutes, they waited. Ben had warned them that Jayden had changed, but when he and Ben walked through the doors, Tessa gasped. Jayden was taller than Ben! And he looked more like his father than ever.

She stood and held her arms out to him. She'd determined she wouldn't cry, but as he stepped into her arms, tears flowed freely down her cheeks. "Welcome home, Jayden." She wiped her face and then held him at arm's length. "How did you get so tall?"

Jayden shrugged, but a grin had formed on his face. "Must have been the mountain air."

Tessa laughed before she hugged Ben.

"Food poisoning all gone?" He leaned down and kissed her on the lips.

She nodded. "Thank goodness. It was horrible."

Eleanor gave Jayden a big hug, and Telford held his hand out.

Jayden took his hand and shook it.

They agreed to have breakfast and a catch up at the new café Tessa had tried with Stephanie. She assured them it wasn't there she'd eaten bad food.

The next couple of hours passed pleasantly, and Tessa's heart warmed as Jayden engaged in conversation, something he'd rarely done before. He told them all about the Morgan's ranch, and his eyes lit up as he described his and Angie's rides into the mountains. He even told them he'd tried to milk a cow. But what brought tears to Tessa's eyes and an inner glow to her heart was when he shared about giving his life to the Lord.

"I didn't understand what true love was until I gave my heart to Jesus." Jayden's gaze was fixed on his hands wrapped around his glass. He looked up and his gaze travelled between Tessa and Ben, finally settling on his father. "I know now that you love me, but I used to think you were too tough on me and didn't really care about me. I'm sorry, Dad." His gaze shifted. "I'm sorry, Tessa."

Tessa reached out her hand and squeezed his wrist. "Jayden,

it's all okay. We've all grown and changed—we're not the same people we were a year ago, and your dad and I are so proud of you. And you're home, that's all that matters." She turned her face away and quickly blinked back tears. She swallowed hard before continuing. "We have a lot of catching up to do, but there's no hurry."

Jayden nodded. "You're right, thank you." His face brightened. "Can we go home now so I can see Sparky and Bindy?"

"Sure can," Ben said. "We need someone else to walk them now Tessa's put on so much weight."

Tessa shot daggers at Ben, but then burst into laughter.

"Come on, let's go home."

They all stood. Telford and Eleanor said good-bye, and then Tessa, Ben and Jayden headed home.

CHAPTER 24

*D*uring their stay at the beach, Tessa suggested they drive to Mrs. Trejo's farm for a visit since it was reasonably close by. She'd been praying about the farm, and had a real sense it was the right thing to do. And when she'd seen how animated Jayden had become when he spoke of the Morgan's ranch, any worries he wouldn't like living in the country had disappeared. The only hiccup now was Ben. But Tessa was convinced that when he saw it, and she shared with him her vision for the place, he'd become as excited as she was.

She took him for a short walk through the property, ending up at the wooden bench where the views over the valleys below to the rolling mountains in the distance still took her breath away.

"Do you like it, Ben?"

He slipped his arm around her shoulders and pulled her close. "It's lovely, Tess. It's so peaceful."

"Could you see yourself living here?"

He tilted his head, his forehead creasing. "What do you mean by that?"

She took a deep, slow breath and raised her head. "Well, it's for sale, and I thought we could buy it and build some small cabins on it and develop it as a retreat. Stephanie's got this job working with disadvantaged youth, and she could bring them here, and..."

Ben placed his finger across her lips. "Whoa, Tess, slow down."

"Sorry. You can see I'm excited about it."

"You're not wrong." The sparkle in his eye gave her hope he might share that excitement. "Tell me what you're thinking, but slowly."

"Okay." She smiled at him and then began. "Well, I've always wanted to live in the country. I could see myself as a country vet. And we've been praying about a ministry, and I think it's the perfect place for a retreat. A place where people can come to recharge, to reconnect with each other and with God, and a place where Stephanie could bring the young people she'll be working with to get away from the city for a while." A grin formed on her face. "And I think Jayden would love it. He doesn't want to go back to the same school, and we could get some horses, and maybe a cow or two, and some chickens." She paused. "What do you think?"

Ben shook his head and laughed. "And what do you suggest I do?"

"You can get a job in town— it's not that far, or you could work from home, or you could become 'Retreat Manager'. Or all of the above!"

He pulled her close and kissed the side of her head. "You've thought of everything, haven't you?"

She nodded.

"Guess we'd better make an offer, then."

Tessa's face expanded into a broad smile as she threw her arms around his neck. She drew back and met his gaze. "Does that mean you're not going to think about it for three months? Or run the figures through your spreadsheets, or even pray about it?"

He chuckled. "We should pray about it, and maybe I'll run some figures, but if we sell our house, I can't see it's a problem." He turned his gaze to the mountains. "Besides, I could easily get used to this. It's the perfect place to raise our family."

Tessa rested her head against his shoulder and sighed. "I can just imagine it. Happy children running around playing games, going fishing, riding horses, getting dirty." She laughed.

"Sounds amazing." He kissed the top of her head and pulled her close.

THE DEAL WAS DONE. The house at New Farm sold quickly, and they'd be moved in by Christmas. Jayden was excited that he'd get his own horse, and he promised to milk the cows every morning. He'd met up with Neil a few times, but they'd both changed, and Jayden was looking forward to making new friends at his new school and new church. Most days he managed to Facetime with Angie, and although it wasn't quite the same, they still laughed together and spent hours talking about everything that was happening in their lives, including what they'd been learning in the Bible study they were doing together. Jayden didn't know when he'd see her again, but he looked forward to the day he would.

TESSA'S BABY was due any day. Jayden was in his room packing the last of his stuff when she called out from downstairs. He raced down to find her doubled over, holding her stomach. She'd been packing boxes in the living room—he was sure Dad had told her not to do that. Dad was at work, tidying everything up before he finished.

"Are you all right?" He placed his arm lightly on her back. She didn't look all right. She certainly didn't sound all right. What a stupid question.

She shook her head.

"Is it the baby?"

"Yes." Her voice was just a whisper.

"I'll call Dad." He helped her to the couch then dialled Dad's number.

Dad answered straight away.

"Dad, it's Tessa. The baby's coming."

"I'm on my way. I'll be home in ten minutes."

"Okay." Jayden turned to Tessa. "Dad'll be home soon. Is there anything I can do?"

She shook her head. "Everything's ready."

He breathed a sigh of relief. He didn't want to deliver a baby on his own.

Dad arrived and helped Tessa into the car. Jayden went with them. Tessa's parents came and sat with him while Dad went in with Tessa.

"It could be a long time, Jayden." Eleanor patted his thigh.

"Will she be all right?"

"The doctor said everything's fine, so yes, God willing, she will be."

"What do you think she'll have?"

Eleanor chuckled. "I've never got it right yet, so if I say it'll be a boy, it'll probably be a girl."

"So what do you think?"

"A boy."

"Okay, so it'll be a girl." He leaned back in his chair. *A little sister*. He could live with that. Maybe they could call her Angie.

Hours passed. Finally Dad appeared through the double doors with a broad smile on his face. "It's a girl. We have a daughter!"

Eleanor jumped up and gave him a big hug. Telford shook his hand, and then hugged him too.

Jayden hung back, but then Dad stepped forward and wrapped his arms around him. "You have a little sister, Jayden. She's beautiful."

"Can I see her?"

"You sure can."

TESSA SAT IN BED, leaning against her pillows, cradling her new little daughter in her arms. She was perfect in every way. A tiny rosebud mouth, softer than soft skin, a beautifully formed face, long lashes, and a light covering of hair. As her tiny fingers wrapped around Tessa's thumb, Tessa's heart swelled with love.

She looked up when Ben returned with Jayden and her parents.

They all stood around her bed, trying to get a better look. Ben sat beside her on the bed and gazed down at their little baby girl.

"What are you going to call her?" Jayden asked.

Tessa glanced at Ben. "Go on, you tell them."

Ben smiled with pride as he gently stroked the baby's head. "Her name is Naomi Joy Williams."

Eleanor let out a happy sigh. "I love it! And she's beautiful, Tessa." Tears ran down her cheeks.

Tessa held her hand out and smiled. "Thanks, Mum."

"Can I hold her?" Jayden stepped closer.

"Of course. Sit in the chair and Dad will pass her to you."

He smiled. "Thanks, Mum."

Tears pricked Tessa's eyes. How long had she been waiting to hear that? And now she had two children to love and cherish. God was so good. Her heart burst with joy as Jayden cradled his little sister in his arms. Her gaze met Ben's and her spirit soared.

"Dear friends, let us love one another, for love comes from God. Everyone who loves has been born of God and knows God."

1 John 4:7

FROM THE AUTHOR

I sincerely hope you've enjoyed reading *"The True Love Series."* I pray that you weren't only touched by the Tessa, Ben and Jayden's stories, but that you now have a greater assurance that you're loved by the God of Creation, and that you can truly have a personal relationship with Him.

If your interest was piqued by the study the Youth were doing and would like to find out more, there are plenty of great books out there, just do a search for "Apologetics" and choose one that appeals to you. It's so exciting to see just how much proof there is for God's existence, and how science is starting to confirm the story of creation. We don't need to take a blind leap of faith—we can have certainty that what we believe is true, and that God really is there and that His love for us is constant and true. I encourage you to spend time finding out more, so that you are *"Always prepared to give an answer to everyone who asks you to give the reason for the hope that you have. But do this with gentleness and respect."* 1 Peter 3: 15. Amen.

Enjoyed the series? You can make a big difference...

Help other people find this book by writing a review and telling them why you liked it. Honest reviews of my books help bring them to the attention of other readers just like yourself, and I'd be very grateful if you could spare just five minutes to leave a review (it can be as short as you like).

Ben, Tessa and Jayden's story continues in the "Precious Love Series", available now on Amazon.

Make sure you're on my readers' email list so you don't miss notifications of my new releases! If you haven't joined yet, you can do so at www.julietteduncan.com/subscribe/ and you'll also receive a free copy of *"Hank and Sarah - A Love Story"* as a thank you gift for joining.

Blessings,

Juliette

OTHER BOOKS BY JULIETTE DUNCAN

Find all of Juliette Duncan's books on her website:
www.julietteduncan.com/library

True Love Series

Tender Love

Tested Love

Tormented Love

Triumphant Love

Precious Love Series

Forever Cherished

Forever Faithful

Forever His

Water's Edge Series

When I Met You

A barmaid searching for purpose, a youth pastor searching for love

Because of You

When dreams are shattered, can hope be re-found?

With You Beside Me

A doctor on a mission, a young woman wrestling with God, and an illness that touches the entire town.

All I Want is You

A young widow trusting God with her future.

A handsome property developer who could be the answer to her prayers...

It Was Always You

She was in love with her dead sister's boyfriend. He treats her like his kid sister.

My Heart Belongs to You

A jilted romance author and a free-spirited surfer, both searching for something more...

A Sunburned Land Series

A mature-age romance series

Slow Road to Love

A divorced reporter on a remote assignment. An alluring cattleman who captures her heart...

Slow Path to Peace

With their lives stripped bare, can Serena and David find peace?

Slow Ride Home

He's a cowboy who lives his life with abandon. She's spirited and fiercely independent...

Slow Dance at Dusk

A death, a wedding, and a change of plans...

Slow Trek to Triumph

A road trip, a new romance, and a new start...

Christmas at Goddard Downs

A Christmas celebration, an engagement in doubt...

The Shadows Series

A jilted teacher, a charming Irishman, & the chance to escape their pasts & start again.

Lingering Shadows

Facing the Shadows

Beyond the Shadows

Secrets and Sacrifice

A Highland Christmas

A Time For Everything Series

A mature-age Christian Romance series

A Time to Treasure

She lost her husband and misses him dearly. He lost his wife but is ready to move on. Will a chance meeting in a foreign city change their lives forever?

A Time to Care

They've tied the knot, but will their love last the distance?

A Time to Abide

When grief hovers like a cloud, will the sun ever shine again for Wendy?

A Time to Rejoice

He's never forgiven himself for the accident that killed his mother. Can he find forgiveness and true love?

Transformed by Love Christian Romance Series

Because We Loved

Because We Forgave

Because We Dreamed

Because We Believed

Because We Cared

Billionaires with Heart Series

Her Kind-Hearted Billionaire

A reluctant billionaire, a grieving young woman, and the trip *that changes their lives forever...*

Her Generous Billionaire

A grieving billionaire, a devoted solo mother, and a woman determined to sabotage their relationship...

Her Disgraced Billionaire

A billionaire in jail, a nurse who cares, and the challenge that changes their lives forever...

Her Compassionate Billionaire

A widowed billionaire with three young children. A replacement nanny who helps change his life...

The Potter's House Books...

Stories of hope, redemption, and second chances.

The Homecoming

Can she surrender a life of fame and fortune to find true love?

Unchained

Imprisoned by greed — redeemed by love.

Blessings of Love

She's going on mission to help others. He's going to win her heart.

The Hope We Share

Can the Master Potter work in Rachel and Andrew's hearts and give them a second chance at love?

The Love Abounds

Can the Master Potter work in Megan's heart and save her marriage?

Love's Healing Touch

A doctor in need of healing. A nurse in need of love.

Melody of Love

She's fleeing an abusive relationship, he's grieving his wife's death...

Whispers of Hope

He's struggling to accept his new normal. She's losing her patience...

Promise of Peace

She's disillusioned and troubled. He has a secret...

Heroes Of Eastbrooke Christian Suspense Series

Safe in His Arms

SOME SAY HE'S HIDING. HE SAYS HE'S SURVIVING

Under His Watch

HE'LL STOP AT NOTHING TO PROTECT THOSE HE LOVES. NOTHING.

Within His Sight

SHE'LL STOP AT NOTHING TO GET A STORY. HE'LL SCALE THE HIGHEST MOUNTAIN TO RESCUE HER.

Freed by His Love

HE'S DRIVEN AND DETERMINED. SHE'S BROKEN AND SCARED.

Stand Alone Christian Romantic Suspense

Leave Before He Kills You

When his face grew angry, I knew he could murder...

The Madeleine Richards Series

Although the 3 book series is intended mainly for pre-teen/Middle Grade girls, it's been read and enjoyed by people of all ages. Here's what one reader had to say about it: *"Juliette has a fabulous way of bringing her characters to life. Maddy is at typical teenager with authentic views and actions that truly make it feel like you are feeling her pain and angst. You want to enter into her situation and make everything better. Mom and soon to be dad respond to her with love and gentle persuasion while maintaining their faith and trust in Jesus, whom they know, will give them wisdom as they continue on their lives journey. Appropriate for teenage readers but any age can enjoy."* Reader

ABOUT THE AUTHOR

Juliette Duncan is a *USA Today* bestselling author of Christian romance stories that 'touch the heart and soul'. She lives in Brisbane, Australia and writes Christian fiction that encourages a deeper faith in a world that seems to have lost its way. Most of her stories include an element of romance, because who doesn't love a good love story? But the main love story in each of her books is always God's amazing, unconditional love for His wayward children.

Juliette and her husband enjoy spending time with their five adult children, eight grandchildren, and their elderly, long-haired dachshund, Chipolata (Chip for short). When not writing, Juliette and her husband love exploring the wonderful world they live in.

Connect with Juliette:

Email: author@julietteduncan.com

Website: www.julietteduncan.com

Facebook: www.facebook.com/JulietteDuncanAuthor

BookBub: www.bookbub.com/authors/juliette-duncan

Made in the USA
Coppell, TX
27 February 2023

13481780R00125